WHISKEY AND GUNPOWDER

An Addison Holmes Novel

LILIANA HART

JJ Graves Mystery Series
Dirty Little Secrets
A Dirty Shame
Dirty Rotten Scoundrel
Down and Dirty
Dirty Deeds
Dirty Laundry
Dirty Money
A Dirty Job
Dirty Devil
Playing Dirty
Dirty Martini
Dirty Dozen
Dirty Minds
Dirty Weekend
Dirty Looks
Dirty Liars
Dirty Valentine

Addison Holmes Mystery Series
Whiskey Rebellion
Whiskey Sour
Whiskey For Breakfast
Whiskey, You're The Devil
Whiskey on the Rocks
Whiskey Tango Foxtrot
Whiskey and Gunpowder
Whiskey Lullaby

The Scarlet Chronicles
Bouncing Betty
Hand Grenade Helen
Front Line Francis

The Harley and Davidson Mystery Series
The Farmer's Slaughter
A Tisket a Casket
I Saw Mommy Killing Santa Claus
Get Your Murder Running
Deceased and Desist
Malice in Wonderland
Tequila Mockingbird
Gone With the Sin
Grime and Punishment
Blazing Rattles
A Salt and Battery
Curl Up and Dye
First Comes Death Then Comes Marriage
Box Set 1
Box Set 2
Box Set 3

The Gravediggers
The Darkest Corner
Gone to Dust
Say No More

Laurel Valley
Tribulation Pass
Redemption Road
Midnight Clear
Forgiveness River
Atonement Trail

Dedication

To Scott and the Kids-

This one was truly a family effort.

Scott- Thanks for telling me when the book wasn't funny enough. You pushed it to be the best it could be, and I'm forever grateful. I didn't mean it when I said I wouldn't sleep with you again.

Kids- I love y'all like crazy, even when you run through the house, wrestle, and generally make as much noise as possible while I'm on deadline. I hope you all ate something besides pizza and ice cream while I was in the writing cave.

Prologue

In less than twenty-four hours, I'd be a married woman.

I was no Meghan Markle, but this wedding was kind of a big deal. The *Whiskey Bayou Gazette* had dubbed it the "Wedding of the Decade." If you read past the headline, it was apparent that it was more for titillation than because it was a BFD, as my Aunt Scarlet liked to remind me. It had been alluded to that my hasty nuptials were due to the fact that I was in the family way. Which was the Southern way of saying I got knocked up. I'm not, by the way.

The second not so subtle mention of my nuptials in the *Gazette* referred to my previous wedding. Two hundred people watched me get stood up at the altar the last time, so it seemed like overkill to me to mention it again, but news was slow this time of year.

My name is Addison Holmes, and I have a tendency to make headlines on a fairly frequent basis. I work at the

McClean Detective Agency as a private investigator. My license is still new and shiny, and I had a couple of highly publicized cases under my belt. My skills were improving, and mixing skills with sheer dumb luck seemed to be a winning combination. And my near-death experiences were getting fewer and farther between.

That pretty much brings us up to date and explains why I'm standing in the parking lot of the First United Methodist Church in Whiskey Bayou. My friend, bridesmaid, and sometimes sidekick, Rosemarie Valentine, was with me, along with FBI Special Agent Matt Savage. It was hard to go anywhere without Rosemarie. She was like a puppy, though she was mostly house-trained. As for Savage, I wasn't a hundred percent sure why he was with us, but he wasn't really on board with the whole wedding thing, so I figured that had more to do with it than anything.

"This is like déjá vu," Rosemarie said. "It seems just like yesterday when you were getting married here for the first time."

Savage coughed to cover his laugh, and I gave him the stink eye.

"Thanks for reminding me," I said, shivering beneath my coat. I was almost positive my shivers had everything to do with the weather and not the feeling of impending doom. *Almost.*

It was the coldest winter Savannah had seen in a hundred years. I wasn't one to criticize, except when it was important or about someone I knew, but I was confused by the reports of global warming. It was two degrees, and we were supposed to get snow. A lot of snow. In Georgia. Either Mother Nature was drunk, or Al Gore's tiny jogging shorts had cut off the circulation to his brain.

"Do you think he's really here?" Rosemarie asked. "This place looks deserted. No cars in the parking lot, and his car hasn't moved in three days. It's like an omen."

It did look rather bleak Beverly said he's been in and out. Morning is the best time to catch him. Do you think he'll talk to you?" I asked Savage. The cold must have affected my thinking process because one look at his face made it very clear Savage had no plans to talk to him.

He just smiled at me, like that was going to have any effect on me whatsoever. I mean, sure he had that cute dimple at the corner of his mouth and he was giving me that look he always had right before he wanted to kiss me. But I was an engaged woman, and all that kissing stuff was off the table. He was nothing more than an incredibly hot, muscle-bound…co-worker. Who had a life I knew absolutely nothing about.

"I don't know what's happening here," Rosemarie said. "But I feel like a dark spirit has descended over this place. It's giving me the chills. I say we go home and you can find a new place to get married." She made the sign of the cross and that gave *me* the chills.

"Stop it," I said. "You're not even Catholic. And this has nothing to do with me getting married. He hired me to do a job, and that's what I'm doing."

"Keep telling yourself that," she said, and crossed herself again.

I was feeling the wedding day pressure and Rosemarie had just hit my last nerve. I launched myself toward her. Savage grabbed the collar of my coat like a puppy, and I almost strangled myself.

"Slow down there, tiger," he said. "Are you sure you want to get married?"

"Stop asking me that," I said, shaking myself loose. "You've got to move past me. I know that you're mildly attracted to me, and on another level, I'm sure I give you a glimpse of the lighter side of this job. I know you're mired in the muck of the horrible things people do to one another on a day-to-day basis. And here I am, like a zoo animal, ready to amuse you when you're bored."

"What you're saying is you're a zoo animal I'm mildly attracted to?" he asked.

"Shut up. You know what I mean." I was starting to get flustered, but I was having trouble closing my mouth. "Plus, you're a fantastic kisser. And I'm not so bad myself, so I see the appeal there." For some reason, I wanted to make sure I didn't take away from the compliment I'd just given him about his kissing, so I reinforced it with a, "Really, you're very good."

"I appreciate that," he said, grinning.

Rosemarie was staring at me wide-eyed, as if I'd lost my mind. Maybe I had.

"You just don't seem like the settling down type," I said against my better judgment. "You're very tempting because you have that bad-boy, rule-breaker vibe. And all the crazy socks are weirdly sexy. And then your body…"

I was talking so fast I was starting to deprive my brain of oxygen. Maybe I'd pass out and by the time I woke up the wedding and anything else I could possibly embarrass myself about would be over.

"I'm just saying that you need a woman who gives you hell," I said. "Everything seems to come easy for you, and that includes women. The second I would've given in to temptation you would've dropped me like a hot rock. And then where would I be?"

"Not standing in single-digit temperatures in a church parking lot," he answered.

"Right," I said, nodding.

Rosemarie looked back and forth between the two of us and crossed herself again.

I rolled my eyes.

"What?" she asked. "I like it. I do it all the time. I saw that demon woman Patty Strobel at the Piggly Wiggly fighting over the last roll of toilet paper to prepare for the big storm. I tell you, she was going to punch Maggie Gerber right in the face. And you know Maggie is older than dirt. She would've disintegrated right there on aisle seven. But I made the sign of the cross and cast out the demon. Patti collapsed right there at Maggie's feet."

"That's because Maggie tased her. She had burn marks right in the center of her chest."

Rosemarie hmmphed and gave me the side eye. "I'd expect that from an unbeliever. Got an explanation for everything."

"Let's just get this over with," I said. "I'm in a crisis. In case y'all haven't realized it, we don't have a preacher to marry us."

"One person's crisis is another's opportunity," Savage said.

"Is that in the Bible?" Rosemarie asked.

Savage just smiled at her, and she unbuttoned her puffy yellow coat and started fanning herself. I couldn't blame her. Savage's smile was dangerous.

"I have a backup plan," I lied. "Everything is going to be just fine. By this time in a couple of days I'm going to be a married woman."

Rosemarie flipped open her binder and ran a scarlet-tipped finger down the page. "Nope," she said. "At this time tomorrow, you'll be getting your eyelashes put on."

I looked at her, horrified. "I already have eyelashes. What are you going to do with my real ones?"

This wasn't the first time she'd made comments about my wedding day preparations that absolutely terrified me.

"Let's just get this over with," Savage said. "If he's here, I've got to arrest him."

"I don't want any part of that," Rosemarie said. "The people in this town will skin you alive for arresting their favorite pastor. There's got to be some rule about that somewhere. Are you allowed to arrest a man of God?"

Savage just stared at her blankly. "He's a murderer."

"I'm just saying, I think it's best if maybe we don't associate with you after the arrest. We want people to still come to the wedding."

Savage took his gun out of his holster and held it down by his side in case anyone passed by. The citizens of Whiskey Bayou weren't exactly known for being subtle.

Rosemarie was right. I was going to be the most hated woman in Whiskey Bayou. Everyone loved Pastor Charles.

I was carrying my Glock concealed, but it wasn't worth the trouble of undoing all my winter gear to get it out. Between Savage and my goose down, I figured I was practically bulletproof.

Rosemarie and I followed Savage up the front steps to the big wooden double doors of the church. My heart hammered in my chest, and I was having a little trouble breathing. The truth was, I hadn't stepped foot in this church since my previous wedding debacle.

Savage put his hand on the heavy iron knob and turned to look at me. "You okay? You look a little green."

"I'm all good. Nothing but happy thoughts about this place. I'm getting married. Nothing is going to dampen that excitement."

"That's the spirit," Rosemarie said. "You just put all that other junk out of your mind. The past is in the past. I bet no one even remembers that you got left at the altar, or that they found your fiancé butt naked in the back of your honeymoon limo." She giggled and then put her hand over her mouth. "I've still got the newspaper clippings in my scrapbook. They put those little smiley faces right over his junk and plastered him all over the front page."

Savage's lips twitched and I could see the laughter in the crinkle of his eyes.

"Why are you bringing all this up if you think no one is going to be talking about it?" I asked Rosemarie.

She shrugged. "I don't know. Every time I walk into this church it's the first thing I think about. It's like I can't help myself. You're always good for headlines."

"Are we going to stand out here and reminisce all day?" I asked.

"It's almost worth it," Savage said with a sigh.

He opened the door and slipped into the dim foyer, and Rosemarie and I went in behind him. It took a couple of seconds for my eyes to adjust, but everything looked the same. Marble floors, stained-glass windows, and weird wood-and-iron light fixtures that would instantly impale anyone if they fell from the ceiling.

The doors to the sanctuary were closed, and it felt like the church was completely empty. But a shiver still ran down my spine.

Savage slowly opened the sanctuary doors and we filed onto the red carpeted aisle. I could smell the linseed oil they used to polish the pews and the musty pages of the hymnals. Light filtered in from the floor-to-ceiling, stained-glass windows, and there was a giant cross that hung above the baptismal at the back of the pulpit.

My heart sank, and I looked over at Rosemarie. She crossed herself and held out her fingers in the sign of the cross toward me.

"No offense," she said. "But you have the worst luck."

I wish I could've argued with her, but she was right. There was a body hanging on the cross, and it didn't belong to Jesus.

"Well," Savage said. "Looks like you're going to have to postpone the wedding after all. This is officially a crime scene."

Chapter One

MONDAY

My mother liked to say that the Lord worked in mysterious ways, and I'd have to agree with her on that one. In fact, I was pretty sure the Lord was working overtime in the mysterious department where I was concerned. There was no other way to explain why Pastor Charles Whidbey was sitting in my office at the McClean Detective Agency.

"I need your help," he said. He sat stiffly in the straight-backed chair in front of my desk, his hands clamped together tightly in his lap and his back ramrod straight.

Pastor Charles was probably in his mid-fifties, and he'd been the pastor at the First United Methodist Church in Whiskey Bayou for the last ten years. He was dressed casually—khaki slacks, black turtleneck, and a shabby sport coat with patches on the sleeves. He wore round, wire-rimmed glasses and had piercing blue eyes. His hair was dark, but there was a hint of silver at the temples. He was also ripped as hell. I was guessing when he wasn't praising the Lord he was spending the rest of his time at the gym.

Pastor Charles looked like he might be of some Hispanic descent, but no one really knew much about him. He'd come from another church somewhere in Kansas or Nebraska, and he'd come alone. No wife or kids to speak of, and no relatives that ever came to visit. He'd occasionally share meals in various homes when invited, but for the most part he stayed to himself. He never dated, and the only cause he created for gossip was the lack of a reason for gossip.

"I don't understand," I said. "You need to hire the agency?"

I felt sorry for him. I wondered if in all the time he'd lived in Whiskey Bayou he'd ever grown close to anyone.

"Not exactly," he said, and embarrassment colored his cheeks. "I was hoping we could work out some sort of trade. I don't have the kind of money it takes to hire an agency like this one. But what I do have is an available church on Friday night. I hear you're getting married?"

After the past couple of years had given me some hard knocks, I'd mostly given up on being a religious person. But this was a miracle. Plain and simple. There was no other explanation for it.

"You're saying Nick and I can use the church to get married on Friday, and have the reception there, in exchange for helping you?"

"Yes, that's right," he said, nodding.

"You would marry us?"

"Of course," he said. "Your mother is still a member and attends faithfully. And I was going to perform your last wedding if you remember."

"It's hard to forget," I said, rolling my eyes.

"All things happen for a reason," he said. "Just like the church becoming available at the last minute. Maybe it happened because this was the wedding you were supposed to have all along."

"Oh," I said. I had the overwhelming urge to burst into tears and felt them welling up in my eyes. I blinked rapidly to try and cut them off at the pass.

"Wedding hormones," I said. "It's been a crazy week."

"So I've heard," he said. "You've been making quite a few headlines in the Savannah papers the last month or so."

I grimaced. I'd stopped reading the papers whenever I solved a high-profile case. Especially if I was naked when I cracked a case. My last two cases had ended up with me naked. I was trying to end that streak.

"I imagine with as fast as everything is happening you need as much help as you can get. I saw the open invitation in the *Gazette* this morning. You might have a couple hundred people show up."

"There was an open invitation in the paper?" I asked, wide-eyed.

"Oh," he said. "I'm sorry. I thought you'd placed it there."

"No," I said. "It was probably my mother."

"Or someone who hopes your wedding causes another spectacle."

That sounded ominous, but I guess it wasn't out of the question.

"Don't worry about it," he said. "It'll be a wonderful celebration. John and Edna Korbel were supposed to have their sixtieth anniversary party that night, but they decided to go to Jamaica instead, just the two of them. They said they had too few years left to try and please everyone but themselves, so they'd go celebrate alone."

I blew out a breath, envious of the Korbels' moxie. But they didn't have Phyllis Holmes and Nina Dempsey to deal with.

"Can we serve alcohol at the reception?" I asked.

"We're not Baptists," he said, smiling a little. "A wedding is a celebration. Enjoy it."

"You've got a deal," I said.

Technically, what I'd just done was completely against agency policy. I wasn't supposed to take on private cases, but since this one wasn't for actual money, I was pretty sure I could convince Kate that the loophole would stand up in court. Or she could just fire me, but she was my maid of honor, so I figured the chances were slim. Though Kate *was* a stickler for the rules.

I'd deal with it later. I took out a legal pad from my desk

drawer and grabbed a pen. "What can I help you with?" I asked.

"I've been receiving threats," he said calmly.

This was not what I'd been expecting at all. "Threats," I said. "Why wouldn't you go to the police?"

He reached inside his sport coat and took out an envelope. "I'd prefer to keep this quiet. You know there are no secrets in Whiskey Bayou. It could be a prank, but it could also be something more serious. There's no need to draw attention to it unless absolutely necessary. That could be what they want."

I took the envelope from him. It was a standard size white envelope and inside were several photographs. I looked through them one by one. Obviously, someone had been following Pastor Charles and taking pictures of him without his knowledge.

"Where did they leave the pictures?" I asked.

"Here and there," he said. "A couple in the front seat of my car. Some in my office at the church. And the last one I found on my nightstand this morning."

I looked at the last photograph. It was a picture of Pastor Charles sleeping in his bed.

"Scary," I said.

"To say the least," he agreed.

"When did they leave the first pictures?" I asked.

"A couple of weeks ago. And then I would get more every three or four days."

"Whoever's been watching you has been doing it for a while," I said, turning one of the photographs around. "There's still leaves on the trees at the park, and there are people out and about, so the weather wasn't too cold. So we're looking at least at late fall."

"I see," he said, nodding slowly, and the color seemed to drain from his face. "I missed that. So they've been watching me for months. And now they've decided to play with me."

"Are you sure the police isn't the better option here? At least until you know if you're in any real danger."

"No." He shook his head rather adamantly. "I'm sure about that. I don't want the police involved. I support law enforcement, of course, but they have much more important matters to deal with."

"Have you received anything else?"

"A couple of phone calls where no one was on the other line. And a note stuck to my car window."

"What did it say?" I asked.

"Remember."

"Remember what?"

"That, I don't know," he said. "I'm fifty-eight years old. I've got a lot of life behind me. It could be anything."

"Have you ever had any disagreements or complaints within the church?" I asked. "Unhappy congregation?"

"Nothing out of the ordinary," he said. "Of course, people will come and go from the church. They might disagree with my teaching, or there might be a squabble or so inside the congregation. I've had couples angry because I refused to marry them if I felt they weren't ready. But nothing egregious or that stands out in my mind."

"What about personnel? Anyone let go or hired recently?"

"Pastor Elaine is our newest hire, and she's been with the church for five years now. My secretary and the custodial staff have been there since long before I came to Whiskey Bayou."

"What about your previous church? I was told you came here from the Midwest?" I was straddling a line between professional and personal curiosity.

His lips pressed together and he nodded. "Yes, from a small town outside of Omaha. But I'm afraid my life just hasn't been that exciting."

"Do you have a card?" I asked. "With your cell number? I might have some more questions once I start investigating. When I find out who's doing this, what do you want me to do?"

"Just give me the identity," he said. "Maybe they'll listen to reason if I speak to them face to face."

Or you could get your head bashed in. But I decided not to say that out loud.

Pastor Charles took his wallet from his back pocket and opened it, revealing a thin stack of business cards with the church's logo on it. He handed me one and I paper-clipped it to the pad I'd been writing on.

"I'm sure I don't need to tell you to be careful," I said. "But I'm going to anyway. Don't take any unnecessary chances. Make sure you lock your doors and windows at night. Be vigilant when you go out. Let me know immediately if you think someone is following you, or if you recognize anyone."

"It seems quite foolish for anyone to try and attack me," he said. "Everyone knows me, and I'm out in the community all the time."

"Speaking of, do you have a day-to-day routine? Do you go to the same places or take the same routes every day?"

"Ahh," he said, nodding his head. "I see. Yes, I do for the most part. Unless someone is sick or I need to make a hospital visit or bury someone."

"Could you text me your schedule?" I asked. "It's more than likely that whoever is doing this knows your schedule as well as you do."

"Sure, I'll send it over as soon as I get back to my office. Today is my off-day," he said, and then smiled and pointed up to the ceiling. "There's never really an off day doing His work."

I smiled, but it was forced. I was really worried about Pastor Charles. If someone had taken a picture of me sleeping and left it on my nightstand, I would've been inconsolable.

"Please be careful, Pastor Charles," I said and shook his hand.

He squeezed my hand and placed his other hand on top of mine. And then he looked me in the eyes, and I realized there was a lot more depth to Pastor Charles than I'd ever realized.

"I have faith," he said. "Do you?"

He released my hand and then he was gone, leaving me alone in my tiny office. I sat back behind my desk and made a new file for Pastor Charles, putting my notes and his pictures inside, along with his business card. I lingered over it a little longer than normal because it kept my mind off of the wedding.

The minute I started thinking about it again the pressure returned to my chest and I had trouble breathing. I tried to stick my head between my knees, but there wasn't enough room to maneuver between my desk and the wall.

I pounded on my chest and realized I was more than likely having a panic attack. Or maybe a heart attack. The pressure in my chest had reached epic proportions, and the Costco-sized bottle of Tums I'd bought a couple of days ago sat empty on my desk.

I scooted off my chair and crawled to the front of my desk where there was a little more room, and I laid flat on my back and sucked in deep breaths. I found it only slightly ironic that Pastor Charles had asked if I had faith less than fifteen minutes ago, and here I was about to meet my maker.

The really ironic thing was that I was about to die just like my dad. Of course, I wasn't screaming at the television during a Falcons game, but I did have a pile of open cases on my desk, a boatload of stress, and a half-eaten éclair within arm's reach, so it was mostly the same.

The only difference was I was going to die in my little office at the McClean Detective Agency. Alone. In a space that had been a janitor's closet until I'd taken the initiative to clean it out and claim it as my own. No one would ever find me. At least, not until the smell of decomposition overpowered the scent of the fresh baked goodies that were constantly being delivered from the bakery down the street. I'd gained four pounds since I'd passed the physical fitness portion of the private investigator's test.

A whimper escaped my mouth, and a tear trickled out of the corner of my eye. I was feeling downright sorry for myself now that the chest pains were subsiding.

What I needed to do was focus on work and not on the fact that I was getting married in five days. It wasn't even the idea of marriage that was giving me heart palpitations. I loved Nick and I was ready to take the next step in our lives.

No, the problem was that I was tethered by Southern etiquette and a bunch of crazy women I was supposedly related to. I haven't run a DNA test yet, so there's still hope I'm adopted.

It had been three days since I'd agreed to become Nick's wife. He'd been very patient over the last month while he waited for my decision on whether or not I was going to marry him. So I couldn't really blame him for my newfound arrhythmia.

He'd given me the choice of eloping or having a week to plan a wedding so our family and friends could be involved. Then he'd gotten called out to a triple homicide in the middle of the night and I hadn't seen him since. The lucky duck.

Nick was a good man, and he really did love me. But I'd needed the time to decide if he was the right man for me. He was a cop. And I was the daughter of a cop. But I knew from watching my parents' marriage that there was a whole lot of extra baggage that went with being a cop's wife. My parents had survived their marriage, but that's the best thing I could say about it. I didn't want to end up like that.

I'd made my decision to get married, and I wasn't turning back. I'd been all for the elopement option, but the thing about Southern etiquette was it also included Southern guilt. My mother would never let me hear the end of it if we ran off to some island paradise and exchanged vows without her and half of Whiskey Bayou present. So I'd decided the right thing to do was put together a smallish wedding for close friends and family. Only I must have been in denial because the days were ticking away and I hadn't done one blessed thing to plan for it except ask Kate to be my maid of honor.

Except now it wasn't a smallish wedding at all because Pastor Charles had seen an open invitation in the *Whiskey*

Bayou Gazette. Though I did have a venue for the ceremony and reception, so that was a check in the plus column.

I figured the best thing to do was deal with the rest later. I'd have either died from the heart attack by then or thought of a way to get everything done for the wedding *and* clear all my cases.

I rolled to my hands and knees and boosted myself up, and then I gathered the case files on my desk. The faster I started working, the sooner I'd clear them. I shoved them into my oversized Kate Spade travel bag. It was hot-pink, and the splash of color broke up the gloom surrounding me. I wore jeans, a fitted black sweater, and black Yves Saint Laurent galoshes that came almost to my knees. They were quilted on the inside and worth every penny.

I'd gotten a reward a couple of weeks ago for catching the Romeo Bandit, and it had fattened my bank account quite nicely. I'd bought the boots, the bag, and a giant custom van that was perfect for stakeouts and quickies. I knew both of these things from experience. It even had a bathroom and tiny kitchenette.

My bank account was back to empty again after my extravagant purchases, which meant I had to get back to solving the cases I'd been assigned. Nick was rich. His whole family was rich. But I wasn't marrying Nick for his limitless bank account, though I did enjoy the little BMW convertible he'd bought me as a surprise. I had principles, but I wasn't stupid.

My mother always said to never look a gift horse in the mouth. When I was a kid I'd thought the saying was never *lick* a gift horse in the mouth. As an adult, both sayings make about as much sense as the other to me. I still don't know what a gift horse is or why I'd want to look at it or lick it.

I grabbed my holster from the hook on the back of my door and strapped it around my waist, and then went through the process of putting on my pink-and-black plaid scarf. I hated winter. Everyone in the South hated winter. And we were in the midst of record-breaking temperatures. Southerners weren't meant for single-digit temperatures and snow. No one knew how to dress or drive, and at the first mention of the word snow, people flooded the grocery stores and bought out all the toilet paper and condoms.

I took my black puffy coat from the hook and was just about to put it on when there was a knock at the door. I thought about not opening it and pretending I wasn't there.

"It's me," Kate said. "I can hear you breathing."

I opened the door and came face to face with Kate McClean. She'd been my best friend for as long as I could remember, and we were about as opposite as two people could get, but it seemed to work for us. She was a couple of inches over five feet and cute as a button. She looked a little like Meg Ryan before Meg had made so many poor plastic surgery choices, and her blonde hair came just below her chin and was slightly tousled.

Kate was one of the most no-nonsense people I'd ever known. She said what she meant and meant what she said, and you could always count on her for loyalty and the truth. It's how she'd made such a success out of the agency after she'd quit being a cop after a couple of years.

"Could you really hear me breathing?" I asked.

"No, but your van is still parked out front, and there's fresh cinnamon rolls in the break room. I know you can't smell them from in here, so I figured you were in here hiding."

"That's good detective work."

"That's why they pay me the big bucks."

As soon as I stepped into the hallway the smell of freshly baked cinnamon rolls assaulted my senses and my mouth began to water.

"That's just cruel," I said. "I'm supposed to get married on Friday. They're going to have to roll me down the aisle."

Kate arched her brow and didn't say anything.

"I'm still going to have one," I clarified. "I just want you to know it's cruel."

"Duly noted," she said. "Cute bag. You off to do wedding stuff?"

"Sure," I lied. "I'm also hoping to catch Matt Martin and his nooner. It's not always easy to find parking for the van, so I want to give myself plenty of time."

"Good thinking," Kate said, but she seemed distracted.

I followed her down the hallway to the conference room and had an out-of-body experience the second I could see who was waiting for me. Even though my brain hadn't quite registered what I was seeing, my body kept moving until I was inside the room and it was too late to escape.

"What fresh hell is this?" I hissed at Kate.

"This is what's called a necessary evil. And as your maid of honor, it's my job to make sure things get done. No arguments. We're going to kick this wedding's ass."

"You're fired," I said, panic starting to take hold of me. I felt the pressure in my chest again and was sure this time my heart was really about to explode.

"You can't fire me," she said, entirely too smug. "But this needs to be done. You have work and I'm stuck testifying in court most of the week. Everyone else is working overtime so you can take the next two weeks for your honeymoon, so suck it up. What you're about to witness here is my genius, so sit down in that chair and let's get this over with."

I shook my head slowly. "Do you even realize what you've done? None of us might escape here alive."

"Don't worry," she said, giving me a shove toward the giant conference table. "I've got my taser if things go downhill."

"You think a taser is going to stop them?"

"What's all that whispering about?" Aunt Scarlet yelled from her place at the head of the table. "I don't have all day. The police are on my tail and I could die at any moment. I'm an old lady."

"Demons never die," my mother said under her breath.

This was my own personal hell. My family managed to coexist by never being in the same room at the same time. It had worked that way for generations. The Holmeses were avoiders. If there was a conflict or disagreement, we were pros at burying it deep inside so we could gripe about it to someone who didn't share blood at a later time.

"I'm not going to lie," Kate whispered. "I've never experienced this kind of terror."

"That's very helpful. And this is all your fault. God's going to punish you."

"You don't think standing in this room is punishment enough? I'm not even related."

"Good point," I said.

The conference room was where we had our weekly case briefings, and also where we brought clients we didn't feel a hundred percent comfortable with. It was hooked up with cameras and audio. Just in case.

There was a marble fireplace against one wall, and a fire crackled soothingly in the hearth. The cinnamon rolls sat untouched in the middle of the huge rectangular conference table. Twelve plush chairs sat around it. Three of the chairs were occupied by my family—my mother, sister, and Aunt Scarlet.

Scarlet sat at the head of the table like a general. I personally liked Aunt Scarlet, but she was best had in small doses. I'd shut down a black market organ harvesting ring the week before, and Aunt Scarlet had helped in a big way. I was also almost positive that she'd murdered the man who'd masterminded the whole thing. Ugly Mo had been a crime boss for more than two decades in Savannah, and even the police hadn't been able to touch him. But I was proud to say that with my training and a whole lot of dumb luck, we'd cracked the case.

It didn't change the fact that the police wanted to talk to Scarlet since she was a person of interest. But the last I'd heard, she'd skipped town and was heading back to the cruise ship she lived on for a good part of the year. I was pretty surprised to see her.

She'd changed her hair over the weekend. Gone was the white helmet of curls that had sat so rigidly on her scalp. She'd at least had the appearance of looking like anyone's eccentric grandma with that hair. But now her hair was a cross between Blac Chyna and Bette Davis in *Watcher in the Woods*.

She had it pulled up into an artful ponytail that trailed halfway down her back. Little wisps of hair framed her wizened face, and the white seemed brighter than normal. The bulk of it was almost half the size she was. I didn't know how she was holding up her head.

My mother sat to Scarlet's right. I was pretty much the spitting image of my mother, which was good news for me because my mom was aging well. Her hair was dark like mine and pulled into a messy bun on top of her head. Her eyes were dark and the only signs of aging were the small lines around her eyes.

Mom was in her mid-fifties and starting a new life. She'd recently gotten married to my dad's old partner, Vince

Walker, and they seemed very happy. She'd also started to come into her own a little. I hadn't realized how repressed she'd been during her marriage to my dad. It was nice to see her blooming, but also terrifying at times. My mom no longer had a filter. I hoped Kate had her taser on high stun.

Mom had started going to pottery classes and naked yoga, and she'd set a bonfire in the backyard to burn all her pantyhose and suits from her days as a CPA. She mostly did people's taxes now in yoga pants or overalls. I was still getting used to it.

A fourth chair was occupied by Rosemarie Valentine. She was my other bridesmaid and had a giant binder sitting in front of her. She looked terrified and was pale as a piece of paper.

"I guess the newspaper article is true," Scarlet said, looking me up and down and then zeroing in on my middle. "I guess we're getting another seven-month baby in this family."

I sucked in my stomach and narrowed my eyes. "I'm not pregnant. It's winter. Layers make everyone look heavier."

Scarlet hmmphed and shook her head. "That's the problem with people nowadays. Their scandals are boring. Nobody cares about seven-month babies. Your great-great-uncle sired half the babies in Whiskey Bayou back in his day, but it was his wife that made headlines." Her eyes were animated and she clicked her tongue in approval. "Maudine had enough of his tomcattin' around and cut his doo-dad right off. Stuck it in a jar of vinegar on her windowsill like some lumpy potato. I saw it for myself when I was a kid.

She watched him bleed out while she ironed the rest of his shirts, bless her soul. Of course, she was a Holmes too, and Holmes women don't handle being cuckolded well. Just look at you and how you ran over that fiancé of yours. I was real proud of you. I read about it in the newspaper on my cruise ship."

I opened my mouth to deny any wrongdoing. It's not like I ran over him on purpose. But my sister Phoebe's gasp drew everyone's attention.

"Wait a second," she said. "How could our great-great-uncle's wife be a Holmes too? Are you saying they were related?"

Everyone scrunched up their noses in disgust, and Rosemarie took the opportunity to reach for a cinnamon roll.

I hadn't seen Phoebe in a few months. She was an artist, so she tended to not put down roots in any one place for very long. She was a few inches shorter than me, had long blonde hair with turquoise streaks, and a diamond stud in her nose. She was wearing a black skinsuit that looked like it was made of rubber and a pair of biker boots that came up to her knees.

"Third cousins, so it hardly counts," Scarlet said. "And they didn't have any children. Probably for the best since they were both batshit crazy. The population was a lot smaller then, and men weren't easy to come by. Fortunately, they also didn't live as long so no one had to suffer for too long."

"Sweet Jesus," my mother said. She had a to-go cup of something in front of her, and I was guessing it wasn't hot coffee, because she took a long drink and looked a lot more relaxed when she put the cup down. She glanced at Rosemarie's half-eaten cinnamon roll and reached for her own.

"I'm not pregnant," I repeated to get things back on track. "Nick is just tired of waiting. We want to get this done as quick as possible with as little hassle."

"Hmmph," Scarlet said. "That's just what your mother said before she and your father got married."

My mom rolled her eyes. "How many times do I have to tell you that I got pregnant on our honeymoon. We didn't have to get married. Phoebe just came two months early."

"So you said at the hospital when you were trying to explain to anyone who would listen how a seven-month baby could weigh nine pounds."

"Damn," Kate whispered. "Burn."

"You changed your hair," I said to Scarlet, mostly because I couldn't think of anything else to diffuse the tension between her and my mother.

"I got extensions," she said. "Costs a fortune and they're heavy as hell. But Chermaine told me long hair is back in style, and you know how I'm always on top of the trends."

Chermaine was Scarlet's very expensive stylist. She was… unique.

"Can you believe women half my age are dyeing their hair white on purpose? People are idiots."

My mother snorted. "The women half your age still have

white hair naturally," my mother said. "You're older than dirt."

"The musket ball in my hip may slow me down some, but my hearing's as good as ever, Phyllis. If you weren't family I'd have ripped out that forked tongue of yours decades ago."

I knew things were escalating fast and that I should probably step in before punches were thrown, but I was still stuck on what Aunt Scarlet said about long hair being in style.

"Wait a second," I said, touching the fringe of my new pixie cut. "A week ago you told me I needed a change and Chermaine said short hair was all the rage. I had long hair. Why would you do that to me?"

I wasn't an irrational person. I didn't overreact. Well, maybe sometimes I did, but only when there was a good reason. But I could feel my blood pressure spike and my eyes bulge out of my head. It was wedding stress. It had to be. I was turning into Bridezilla.

Scarlet shrugged. "I can't help it. I'm programmed to eliminate the competition. I thought I had a shot with that hottie, and I could tell he was into you."

"Of course he's into me," I yelled. "We're getting married." I marched over to the table and grabbed a cinnamon roll. To hell with wedding diets.

"Not that one," Scarlet said, waving her hand dismissively. "The other one. With all the muscles and the cute butt.

Looks dumber than he is. I was always a sucker for a jock with a brain. How's his package?"

I shoved the cinnamon roll in my mouth so I didn't have to answer.

Phoebe laughed and knuckle-bumped Aunt Scarlet. "You've got good taste. That man is hot. I thought about giving him a spin myself, but I don't poach. And I don't think he was interested. I can always tell when a man is interested."

"Maybe he's gay," Scarlet said. "Or maybe he has one of those micro-penises and he's too embarrassed to get naked. I read all about micro-penises in *Cosmo*. Apparently, it's much more common now because of all the hormones that get pumped into our foods."

"Kill me now," my mother said.

Rosemarie hadn't said a word, but she was eyeing a third cinnamon roll like it was the Holy Grail and she was the last Templar knight.

Scarlet reached down and plopped her giant Louis Vuitton handbag on the table. She dug around inside and pulled out her checkbook.

"That settles it," Scarlet said. "I'm hiring this agency. Addison, it's your duty to find out if he has a micro-penis. It's dishonest for him to present himself as an eligible bachelor if he can't perform in the bedroom."

"Available to whom?" my mother asked. "You think your fake hair is going to make you look sixty years younger?

One look at you naked would probably turn him off sex forever."

"You've always been jealous, Phyllis," Scarlet said, shaking her head. "I've got the best body money can buy. Addison and Rosemarie can attest to that. We spent all week at that nudist colony. I was fighting men off like flies. Hell, Addison and I are practically twins. She's the spitting image of me."

"I want to die," I said, and Kate patted me on the back soothingly.

"I'm so sorry," she whispered.

My mother shot me a look that somehow managed to look horrified and disappointed in my life choices at the same time.

"It was for a case," I said, defending myself.

Between the nudist colony and being kidnapped and almost having my organs harvested, I figured it was best to keep things on the down-low until life got back to normal. Mom tended to worry. I had no idea why.

"Aunt Scarlet's been here two weeks and look at what an influence she's had on you," my mother said, her voice getting higher as she spoke. "You're not Mata Hari, Addison Holmes. For all we know, all those stories about being a spy and dead husbands and musket balls are complete hogwash. There's no proof of anything other than the fact that she got shipped off to France for being a whore."

We all gasped and I nudged Kate in the side. "Do something. This is your fault. Get out your taser."

"I might have underestimated the outcome of this meeting."

"I'll take the case," I blurted out, hoping it would distract everyone and prevent an all-out brawl. "I'll find out if he has a micro-penis and put in a good word for you if he's… healthy," I said for lack of a better word.

I already knew Savage didn't have a micro-penis. We'd kissed a time or two when Nick and I were in our off-again stage, but that's as far as it had gone. The thing about kissing is it does things to a man's body that's hard to miss, and I could say with certainty that Savage most definitely did not have a micro-penis.

Someone knocked, but the door was open, so it was only for formality. Everyone at the table got unusually still and Rosemarie choked on her cinnamon roll to the point my mother had to slap her on the back a few times.

"Is this a bad time?" Savage asked.

I closed my eyes and wished I could sink into the floor. There was no way he hadn't heard part of that conversation.

"Speak of the devil," Scarlet said, giving him a wink.

Savage moved in next to me and squeezed my shoulder, but I couldn't bring myself to look at him. I was so tense I was surprised I didn't snap in two.

"What are you doing here?" I asked.

"I came about a case, but figured I'd stay for the sideshow."

"Get your money's worth?"

I could practically feel his grin.

"More than," he said. "And it's not even noon yet."

"We're having a meeting about the wedding," Scarlet told him. "She's getting married Friday. Do you have a date?"

"I always go to weddings alone," Savage said. "I like to keep my options open."

"Good thinking," Scarlet said. "Options are important. I've always said that just because you get married doesn't mean you're dead. Lordy, I've been through five husbands. You've always got to be on the lookout for the next one because husbands have a tendency to die or get shot or pushed off balconies. They're very fragile."

I snuck a look at Savage and his grin grew wider. My mom took another drink from her to-go cup, and Rosemarie took another cinnamon roll. We all dealt with stress in different ways.

"Speaking of the wedding," Savage said. "The NAD Squad would like to know where to send their gift."

I sucked in my cheeks. Before I moved in with Nick I was the owner of a cute little white house on an older street in Savannah. It turned out that Savage was my across the street neighbor, which he'd failed to mention to me when he'd suggested I buy it.

My neighbors had been an eclectic mix of races and ages, and they could give Whiskey Bayou a run for its money in the nosey department. They'd also formed a neighborhood watch group called the NAD Squad. I'd been confused at first until they'd told me NAD stood for Neighbors Against Delinquency.

I couldn't even imagine what a gift from the NAD Squad might be, so I said, "Tell them no gifts, but they're all welcome to attend."

His eyebrows raised at that. "Lesser of two evils, huh?"

"Something like that," I said. "What are you drinking, Mom?"

"Orange juice," she said primly.

Phoebe snorted. "I watched her put a teaspoon of orange juice into that vodka this morning."

"Narc," my mother said, and I raised my brows. I felt nothing but sympathy for my mother. For the first time in my entire life she seemed happy, then she finds out Aunt Scarlet is back in town and her daughter is getting married all in the same weekend.

"I hate to chat and run, but I've got work to do," I said, taking a step backward.

"But what about the wedding?" my mother asked. "Where is it going to be? What about your dress? The catering and reception? It's going to take an army to put this together on such short notice."

Her spelling things out like that weren't exactly helping my heart issues. All I cared about was being Mrs. Nick Dempsey.

"Maybe we should elope," I said, and then immediately regretted it when everyone gasped. I had to admit, this was a lot of drama for a Monday morning. Even for me.

"I don't think so," my mother said, looking much too sober for my liking. "There's already been too much publicity. They put out a special edition Sunday *Gazette* yesterday. It's not every day someone from Whiskey Bayou marries a senator's grandson."

"Yes, that's exactly how I describe Nick when I tell people about him. Not that he's out working a triple homicide right now and trying to make the streets safer."

Savage whistled. "He must've caught the Hayward case. You'll be lucky to see him three weeks from now, much less Friday. From everything I've read, that's a messy one."

"Then get out there and help him," I said, smacking Savage on the shoulder. "Because I'm getting married Friday. I don't care who's there or if there are hors d'oeuvres and champagne or Keystone and cake pops. Oh, and by the way, I've secured the Methodist church for the ceremony, and Pastor Charles said we can have the reception there too."

"Is that why he was here this morning?" Kate asked, zeroing in on me. "I was wondering."

It's like Kate had these super mind powers when it came to the agency, and I could practically feel her compelling me to tell her that I'd taken a side job for Pastor Charles.

"Yep," I said, a little too cheerfully. "He said he saw an open invitation in the newspaper this morning, and that the

Korbels had cancelled their sixtieth anniversary party to go to Jamaica, so the church was free."

Technically, I hadn't lied. I just left out the part about the threats.

"Their poor family," my mother said, clucking her tongue. "Their family has been looking forward to that party for months, and then they go off on their own and don't let everyone be a part of the celebration. Those people wouldn't even be there if the Korbels hadn't gotten horizontal back in the day. Maybe they should've thought about that." She gave a soft hiccup and picked at the rest of her cinnamon roll.

"Gross," Phoebe said. "Nobody wants to think about that."

"Are you having an open bar?" Scarlet asked. "Because I don't go to weddings that don't have an open bar. That's just rude. Bad enough I've got to buy you a gift when you'll probably end up getting divorced or one of you dying soon."

Rosemarie came to her feet and slammed her giant binder on the table. She looked scared to death, and while I admired her guts, she had every right to be scared. She was putting herself in the middle of a Holmes family feud. People had died for less.

"Listen up, people," she said. "I took off school today to be here, and I don't want to hear another word about whores, seven-month babies, or micro-penises. We have five days to put on the most spectacular wedding you've ever seen. As friends and family of the bride, it's our job to make sure it goes off without a hitch. And that's exactly what we're going to do.

"I've got everything itemized in this binder, along with a full itinerary. God didn't make Nick rich for no reason, so we're going to use his resources and pull this off. Addison, you've got cases to solve. Go solve them. Savage, you make sure the groom is at the church on time. Whatever you have to do. We've got this."

"Umm," I said.

I'd never seen Rosemarie like this, but she'd just given me my escape and I'd be stupid not to take it.

"Sorry, Kate," I said. "Looks like I've got to run. Have fun."

"I feel like I deserve this somehow," she said.

"Karma's a bitch."

Chapter Two

To my dismay, Savage followed me out of the conference room and into the reception area. Lucy Kim was sitting at the big L-shaped desk that blocked the front waiting area from the offices at the back.

Lucy scared the crap out of me. She'd worked for Kate at the agency since the very beginning, and I was almost a hundred percent sure Lucy was more than just a secretary. But I couldn't prove anything. And if I ever discovered anything I was pretty sure she'd kill me.

She was wearing her customary black pantsuit with red-soled black stilettos. Black concealed blood the easiest, or so I've been told. Her long black hair was pulled up on top of her head and secured with decorative chopsticks. I'd never actually heard Lucy speak. My only conclusion was that she was trying to hide her sharpened incisors.

"Heading out for the day," I told her. "You coming to the wedding Friday night?"

She held up two more files instead of answering.

"Is that a no?" I asked, taking the files and opening them. "You've got to be kidding. I've already got three active cases. Why are you giving me more? When am I going to have time to do wedding stuff?"

She went back to typing away on her computer, her crimson nails clicking a rapid staccato.

I looked at Savage, and he took the files from me and said, "No problem. I just wrapped up a big case and am taking some personal time this week. I'm free to help you."

"Oh, no," I said, shaking my head. "You can't be serious."

"Thanks, Luce," Savage said and then looked at me. "Better put your coat on. It's freezing out there."

I glared at him and gritted out between my teeth, "Yes, I'm aware." But I put on my puffy coat and grabbed my toboggan and gloves from my pocket and put them on.

When he opened the door a shock of cold sliced through my body and took my breath away. It was the most painful thing I'd ever experienced, and that's saying something because I've been shot.

"Don't think that just because you've got a penis and a badge you're going to push me around all day," I said through chattering teeth. "These are my cases and I'm in charge. I've got wedding hormones and I'm feeling real mean today. I'm letting you come with me. Got it?"

"Right," he said, straight-faced. "You won't even know I'm here."

The problem with Savage was he could pretty much get away with anything. He was a beautiful specimen of man, he was smart, and he had a great sense of humor. God wasn't being chintzy on the day Savage was created. He had the kind of chiseled good looks movie stars paid for, and his muscles had muscles. He was Native American, and if I had to guess what his parents looked like, I'd say it was a cross between The Rock and Pocahontas.

I did *not* want to spend the day with Savage working cases. Okay…maybe I kind of did because he was fun, and when he did work cases with me they got solved without me falling out of trees or having to take trips to the emergency room. But Savage was a distraction, and not the good kind. The last thing he wanted was for me to marry Nick. I was a challenge to him. And I wasn't cooperating. I was pretty sure Savage's ego wasn't used to being passed over.

I mean, it's not like Nick is any slouch in the looks and body department. But there's a connection between me and Nick that I've never had with another man before. He's smart, he makes me laugh, and he's a ten on the orgasm Richter scale.

There was no ice or snow on the ground, but the skies were overcast and the clouds fat with the possibility of something ominous. I'd parked my giant conversion van right in front of the agency. It was like a mini-RV, and it blocked the view of Telfair Square and traffic in all directions. I'd started calling her Black Betty on account of she's black and someone had keyed the name Betty above my back left wheel well.

"Want me to drive?" Savage asked.

I sighed. I really did want him to drive. That thing wasn't easy to maneuver in regular traffic, much less downtown Savannah traffic. But at this point all I had left was my pride, and I had to maintain the illusion that I was in control.

"I've got it," I said and clicked the key fob to unlock the doors.

I hoisted myself into the driver's seat and punched in Matt Martin's address on my GPS. I was congratulating myself on my ability to play it cool when I turned the key in the ignition and *I Wanna Sex You Up* blared through the speakers.

I had two choices to make. The first was to frantically turn off the music and look like a fool because Color Me Badd was blaring through my van—a van that had a foldout bed in the back and blue mood lighting for a little romance. Since I'd bought the van from a drug and arms dealer, I couldn't really complain about the enhanced features.

My second choice was to let it play and pretend there was nothing out of the ordinary. I could feel Savage's stare from the corner of my eye, and he was playing a hell of a game of poker, wondering what I'd do next. I shifted my weight in my seat, adjusted my mirrors, and pulled into traffic.

"Interesting choice of music," he said, having to speak a little louder because it was turned up to full volume.

I didn't want to tell him that when I'd parked the car that morning I was listening to Broadway's Greatest Hits so loud it rattled my windows, and I'd forgotten to turn it down before I turned off the car. I didn't need to lose any more cool points with Savage.

"Sorry about that," I said, turning it down. "I was jamming out this morning."

"No worries, happens to me all the time. I figured you more for a show tune kind of girl," he said. "Or maybe big band."

I made a snort of derision and halfway made eye contact, because I enjoyed both of those genres of music. "Nah, man. That's for old people. I'm hip."

What was I doing? Getting married was making me a crazy person. I didn't need to impress Savage. I didn't care what he thought. The only explanation was the wedding hormones. I couldn't imagine what I'd be like by the end of the week.

I pushed the button on the stereo and there was blissful silence from the chorus. Then I took a right on Broughton Street.

"Have you ever been married?" I asked for some inexplicable reason.

Savage looked at me and was thoughtful before answering. It seemed like a pretty cut and dried question to me.

"No."

"That's it?" I asked. "Just no? It feels like there's more there."

The corner of his mouth twitched in what I assumed was a

smile. "You only asked one question. I answered. Where are we going?"

I was going to have to be sneakier if I wanted to get more personal information about Savage.

"The guy's name is Matthew Martin. He lives over on Gaston not far from Nick's parents." I handed him the blue file folder from my bag. "The wife hired us. Thinks he's cheating. They both work from home, but on Monday, Wednesday, and Friday he leaves at eleven forty-five like clockwork and takes the dog for a walk. Doesn't come back home until one-thirty or so."

"Maybe he just likes to have a long lunch with his dog," Savage said, flipping through the file.

There was a headshot of Matthew Martin paper-clipped to the inside of the file folder. He was a middle-aged man with dark hair, a beard, and brown eyes. He was attractive in an average kind of guy way.

"That's what he tells her," I said. "But she found a receipt for a florist in his pants pocket for a box full of rose petals and he didn't buy them for her. And she says he hasn't been interested in her romantically for the last couple of months."

"Yep, that's always a sign. A man has to be almost dead before he goes that long without sex."

I'd known Savage for a year or so, but he'd never talked about dates or other women. So I was naturally curious if he'd been almost dead for the past year or if he'd been getting his kicks elsewhere since I wasn't giving him what he wanted. Not that it mattered in the slightest to me, but I still found myself to be a little perturbed at the notion of Savage with another woman.

I slammed on the brake a little harder than necessary at the intersection just before Gaston, and felt better when Savage jerked against the seatbelt with an *oomph*.

"What's the plan?" he asked.

"I'm getting a feel for his habits. It shouldn't be anything more than easy surveillance. I'll grab a few shots if the moment calls for it, and that's that. We can move on to the next case."

"I can't believe he'd take his dog out for a walk that long in this kind of weather. The wife's right. Something is going on."

"You ever been engaged?" I asked. "Had a long-term girlfriend?"

Savage just smiled. He was mysterious, but it was my new mission to crack him like a nut. I told myself I was doing it for Aunt Scarlet. She'd hired me after all. But in reality, I was just nosy.

I made a pass by Matthew Martin's house. It was a big, pink monstrosity of a Victorian with a small front yard, closed in by a waist-high wrought iron gate.

"That's an ugly house," Savage said.

"Yep, you'd think as much as it probably cost they could afford to make it not look like a cake maker vomited icing all over it."

"Money doesn't buy taste."

"There are a lot of creepy houses in Savannah," I said. "But this one takes the cake." I looked at him out of the corner of my eye. "See what I did there?"

Savage's expression could have cracked stone. "Yeah, good one."

I rolled my eyes and circled the block and came back down the opposite direction.

"I remember you being more fun," I said.

He just smiled in response.

Black Betty wasn't exactly known for her maneuverability and I didn't want to lose my subject while I was doing a twenty-four-point turn in the middle of the street. From what Mrs. Martin had said, her husband always headed toward Forsyth Park when he left on his tri-weekly jaunts, so I parked at the side of the street facing the park. I left the ignition on because I wasn't brave enough to sit in the van without the heat on. I was accustomed to certain creature comforts. Heat was one of them. A working bathroom was another.

I tapped my fingers on the steering wheel, and tried not to make the silence awkward.

"So," I said. "Aunt Scarlet read an interesting article in *Cosmo* the other day."

"I don't have a micro-penis," Savage said.

"Well, then. Case closed. That was an easy one."

"You don't remember?" he asked, arching a brow. "I'm crushed."

I remembered all too well. I felt the heat creeping into my face, so I bent down to grab a bag of trail mix I kept in the little console holder. It had been sitting in the car all night, so the M&Ms were rock hard and shattered in my mouth. But I was committed now and grabbed for another handful so I didn't have to answer.

"Looks delicious," Savage said.

I swallowed the icy shards of nuts and chocolate and managed to look him in the eyes. "Why are you here with me again?"

"Because you're supposedly getting married in four days, and you've got five open cases."

"Six," I said. "I didn't tell Kate everything about Pastor Charles's visit this morning. He traded me the use of the church for the wedding and reception if I'd do a little side job for him. What do you mean *supposedly* getting married?" I narrowed my eyes.

He shrugged. "Anything can happen. I'm here to help. Don't look a gift horse in the mouth."

"Why do people keep saying that? It makes no sense."

"I'm assuming you need to do wedding type stuff this week while you're working your cases. The faster we get this done, the sooner you can do all that." I didn't like the look in his eyes. It was entirely too shifty. "You know...a wedding dress, cake, flowers, rings..."

"Piece of cake," I said. But I was lying.

The pressure was enormous. There was too much to do in too few days, which was why I was procrastinating. When I got overwhelmed I had a tendency to do one of two things: I'd either become a drill sergeant and make everyone's life around me miserable until I accomplished the goal, or I'd become an ostrich and stick my head in the sand, pretending that there were no problems in life and everything was amazing. There was no in between for me.

"Maybe you could help with Pastor Charles," I said, digging in my bag for the file I'd made for his case. "Someone's been tailing him, leaving pictures they've taken in his car and on his nightstand. I can't imagine anyone in Whiskey Bayou doing such a thing, so it's got to be an out-of-towner, but out-of-towners tend to stick out, so surely someone has seen something."

"He hasn't had any trouble?"

I shrugged and repeated everything Pastor Charles had told me. "I don't know…it's just weird. Maybe you could dig around some. The only thing I can say for certain is that he was scared and trying not to show it."

My cell phone rang and it came through the Bluetooth on the stereo. Nick's name flashed across the screen and I blew out a breath.

"Hello," I said.

"I'm heading home for a shower and a couple of hours of sleep."

"I'm sorry, who is this again?"

I heard his sigh through the phone and chanced a look at Savage. He wasn't even trying to be subtle about listening in.

"Sorry I haven't checked in," Nick said. "But cut me some slack. I've been knee-deep in brains for three days."

"I know. I watch the news. I just like to know you're still alive on occasion. Just send me a text with a thumbs up while you're sitting on the toilet."

"But that's when I play solitaire," he said.

"Hilarious. What's up with the case? You wrapping it up?"

"Not by a long shot," he said. "At first glance it looked like a murder/suicide. Husband, wife, and kid. All sitting down for dinner. Husband pulls out gun and blasts wife and kid over dessert. Then he turns the gun on himself. Weapon found at the base of his chair. Residue on his hand from firing the gun."

"But?" I asked.

"The vics were well off. Very well off. They make my parents look like paupers."

"Geez," I said.

"Anyway, the family lives over on Wilmington Island. Huge mansion, gated, security cams and a full staff. The staff had been released after dinner was served, so no one was on the premises."

"Makes sense if the guy was going to off his family," I said.

"Yep, but around seven o'clock there was a blackout and all security glitched off. A system like that isn't supposed to do that if there's a blackout or power surge. For fifteen minutes the entire compound was shut down. We've pulled feed from neighbors' cameras, but haven't found anything there yet."

"Anything taken?" I asked.

"Nothing that we can tell, and all of the staff says everything looks as it's supposed to. The house manager knew where the passwords to the safes were, and all the contents were inside."

I could hear the doubt in his voice. "But?" I asked.

"I'm not buying it. I did a little digging into the vic's tech company. He was about to enter into a merger and release the reins to a new CEO and partners. He'd be a silent member of the board, mostly to keep his name attached to the company and reassure people during the transition, and he'd take the twenty-three billion dollars they were paying him and spend most of his days on the golf course."

"Holy cow," I said. "That's a lot of money."

"Yep, and there's a clause in the contract. If our vic happened to die before the merger took place, they'd only have to pay his estate a hundred million and they'd have full control of everything anyway. Except that the vic's wife and child were his only beneficiaries. Guess what happens to the estate if they die?"

"Everything goes back to the company?"

"Bingo," he said. "Now I just have to prove it."

Nick had a sixth sense about these kinds of cases, and if his gut was saying it wasn't a murder/suicide, then it probably wasn't.

"So…" I said. "Big wedding Friday night." And then I decided to clarify. "Ours."

There were several seconds of silence before Nick said, "How's the planning going?"

"Great," I lied. "Everything will be ready. All you have to do is show up wearing your tux. You have your tux, right?"

I was doing everything I could to not flat out ask him if he'd be able to make it to the wedding. His silence didn't fill me with a lot of confidence.

"I'm about to fall over where I stand," he said instead. "I'm going to chew a roll of Tums, get a couple of hours' sleep, and then piss off some very powerful people. See you in a month or two."

I gasped and he said, "Kidding. Kind of." And then he disconnected.

"It's okay," I said. "He'll figure it out. Just a small speed bump in the road. People get murdered in Savannah every day. They mostly all get solved."

Savage didn't have a reply, which did *not* fill me with a lot of confidence. I decided to get up and make some coffee so I could focus on something besides the wedding for a few seconds.

The little kitchenette was in the back of the van close to the bathroom. It was just a small counter space with a mini-fridge beneath it. But it was enough room for my Keurig. The small cabinet above held a few cups and snacks.

"How do you like your coffee?" I asked.

"Just water for me," Savage said. "I try not to drink caffeine."

I squenched my face up and shook my head. That right there was just one of the reasons Savage and I could never be together. What kind of man could go through life without caffeine?

I grabbed a water from the fridge, but it was frozen solid. I added powdered creamer and sugar to my coffee and then made my way back to the front. I set Savage's water bottle in the cup holder and directed the heater vent on it so it would thaw. We waited another ten minutes in silence.

"I have a good idea," I said. "Why don't we play twenty questions?"

"You think that's a good idea?" he asked, raising a brow in question.

"Sure, we can start with something easy. It's a good way to get to know each other better."

"Why do you want to know each other better?"

"That counts as one of your questions," I said. "But to answer, because we're friends. And friends should know each other. It's good to really get into each other's psyches. Especially when we're working together on potentially life or death situations."

"You think Matthew Martin is a life or death situation?" he asked.

"That's another question," I said. "And of course not. But just over the last couple of weeks, think of all the times I've almost died."

"So you want to be friends with me because you're reckless and I can keep you safe?"

"Technically, that's another question," I said. "You're down to seventeen. You've really got to be careful. It's my turn to ask one. How come you always wear crazy socks?"

"Because I'm not supposed to," Savage said and then he countered with, "Why do you think you've procrastinated so much on this wedding? Do you think it's because subconsciously you don't really want to get married?"

"That's two questions," I said.

"I'm fine with that."

I hunkered down into my seat and crossed my arms over my chest. "I've changed my mind. This game is stupid. We know each other well enough."

Chapter Three

THE NEXT HOUR went by with excruciating slowness. I'd handed Savage all my case files so he could look them over, and he'd had his head buried in them ever since.

"None of these cases are too bad," Savage finally said. "You've got two alleged infidelities, two potential frauds, and a comprehensive background check. I can do that one for you if you want."

"Sure," I said, but I was distracted. I'd spent the last hour mulling Savage's question about why I was procrastinating about the wedding. I decided to call Rosemarie and see if any progress had been made or if there had been any casualties.

I wasn't a technological person, so I had no idea how to take the phone off the Bluetooth setting so it was a private conversation. But I figured we wouldn't be talking about personal things so it probably wasn't that big of a deal. I should've known better.

"What?" Rosemarie barked into the phone. It didn't sound like a cheerful Rosemarie. It sounded like a demon-possessed Rosemarie. But maybe I was projecting.

"I'm just checking in," I said. "How's it going?"

"That question is relative," she answered. "Your mom is wasted and passed out on the table. I can't say I blame her. Scarlet drew a mustache on her with a permanent marker, and your sister just posted it to Instagram. Did you know she has more than a million followers? Is she famous or something?"

"Or something," I said. "Mom is going to kill everyone when she wakes up. She doesn't do hangovers well. The only good news is that she hates social media, so she probably won't see it unless someone shows it to her."

"I don't mean to be critical," Rosemarie said. "But your family is a disaster. They're driving me up the wall. I've eaten a dozen cinnamon rolls. Kate had to call in another order from the bakery."

I couldn't argue with her about my family so I said, "The cinnamon rolls are delicious."

"Kate said she'd take care of getting your mother home, but she's got to testify in court starting this afternoon, so she can't run interference," Rosemarie said. "Scarlet and Phoebe are driving me bananas. They're nosy as hell and have all kinds of opinions." And then her voice dropped down to a whisper. "I had to take your call in the bathroom."

I felt bad for Rosemarie. Despite our rocky beginning, she'd become a good friend, and she was taking more initiative for my wedding than I was. I'd made the choice not to elope, so I needed to suck it up and deal with the consequences of that choice.

"Tell me what I can do to help," I said. "I'm sorry I haven't been more involved. It just seemed too overwhelming."

"That's what friends are for. Between me and Kate, everything will get done. She's good at wrangling all the people into shape and I'm good at pizzazz. This will be the most stress-free week of your life as long as your family stays out of the way. Mostly Scarlet. She tends to be a bad influence."

I sighed. I knew how to keep Scarlet out of the way. "I'll swing by and pick her up around lunchtime. But Phoebe's on her own."

"Thank God," Rosemarie said. "And don't worry about Phoebe. She said something about how the fire crackling in the fireplace gave her a new idea and that she needed to go paint."

"That sounds exactly like Phoebe. Perfect."

"Now that we've got that figured out, we need to talk details. I've got a call in to the church so we can get people in and out for decorating all week. Pastor Charles's secretary is supposed to call me back. I called in some favors and you've got an appointment to try on wedding dresses at Le Couture at six o'clock. Kate and I will meet you there so we can find bridesmaids' dresses. She'll be done with court by then."

"I can't afford Le Couture," I said. "And they have a year-long waiting list to get an appointment."

"Don't be mad," she said, and then she said nothing at all.

The only person I knew who could get a walk-in appointment at Le Couture on such short notice was Nick's mother. I'd rather be skinned alive and roasted on a spit in hell than owe Nick's mother anything. She wasn't nice. Though she was probably the most tolerable of Nick's immediate family. My family drove me crazy, but at least we were a family who loved each other. I had no idea why Nina Dempsey would help us with any part of the wedding. She hated the idea of her son marrying me. And I hated the idea of having her for a mother-in-law, so it equaled out in a way.

"No," I said. "No, no, no."

"You have nothing to worry about," Rosemarie said. "Desperate times call for desperate measures. And Nina Dempsey is a desperate measure. The woman knows everyone in town and can get anything done with the snap of her fingers." Rosemarie was quiet for a couple of seconds and I could hear her chewing. I wondered if she'd snuck a cinnamon roll in the bathroom with her.

"I think she might think I work for her in some capacity. I'm guessing she has a lot of personal staff."

"Good Lord," I said.

"Did you know Nick has open credit at all these wedding vendors? He doesn't even need a credit card. It's like *Pretty Woman*. Except you're not a whore."

"I appreciate that," I said dryly.

"I just tell it like I see it," Rosemarie said. "Just because that Patty Perkins called you a whore when she found out you snagged a hottie like Nick doesn't make it true. She was always jealous of you. I thought she was having an orgasm right in the middle of our staff meeting when the new principal assigned her to take your teaching job. And after you bought your 350Z, she went out and got a red Miata. It's just sad if you ask me."

I was having a hard time remembering who Patty Perkins even was, much less why she'd want to imitate me or be jealous. I peeked over at Savage and saw the quirk of his mouth, even though he was still pretending to read the case files.

"Drop Scarlet at her hotel, and I'll pick her up from there. And then I'll see you at six for the fittings."

"Will do," Rosemarie said. "We've got everything under control. Just hang out with Savage and don't worry about a thing."

I thought about it for a second and then glanced at Savage. His expression was blank, but there was something there.

"Wait a sec…" But Rosemarie had already disconnected.

I turned to Savage. "You're here to babysit me, aren't you?" I asked. "So I don't get in the way."

"I don't know what you're talking about," he said. "The wedding hormones are giving you paranoia. I'm just here to do some legwork and help out a friend in need. Especially since we know each other so well now."

"I sense your sarcasm."

I glanced at the clock. It was almost time for Matt Martin to make an appearance if he was true to schedule.

"Look there," I said. The front door opened and a man fitting Martin's description came out. He was holding on to a leash, and at the other end was an English bulldog dressed in a sweater and knit cap. It was the most ridiculously adorable thing I'd ever seen.

The dog did not look as if it was as enthusiastic to go for a walk as its master, but it lumbered along next to him through the gate and down the sidewalk toward the park.

"Here we go," I said, and put the van into drive. It had gotten nice and toasty during the time we'd been sitting there.

I waited until he got to the corner before I eased out and followed behind him, and if I'd waited too much longer I would have missed him altogether. A yellow taxi sat waiting on the corner on the opposite side of the park, and Matt was lifting his dog to put in the back seat.

"I'm guessing he didn't catch that cab on the fly," I said. It was near impossible to catch a cab around the Forsyth Park unless you'd scheduled a pickup.

"He probably has a standing reservation if he's been doing this three times a week for a couple of months," Savage said.

We wound our way through historic Savannah and out to the highway. I followed behind the cab for about fifteen minutes until they finally took an exit and turned onto a side street.

"Not a great area of town," I said.

"And it's not like you don't blend in," Savage said. "So I'm sure it's fine."

"Again with the sarcasm."

The cab had taken a right down a narrow street with old brick buildings. Windows were broken out and there were bars on any that weren't. The cars in the area were beaten to hell and half of them were missing wheels.

I stopped at the stop sign and idled there, and Savage and I both looked to the right in the direction the cab had gone. It was stopped about halfway down the street, and Matt Martin and his bulldog got out and went to the door of one of the red-bricked buildings. The taxi didn't wait to drive off.

The windows on the bottom floor of the building were boarded up with plywood. I couldn't see who answered the door, but someone must have because Matt and the dog disappeared inside.

"You think if I park the van on that street it'll still be there when we get back?"

"Life's a gamble," Savage said.

"Very helpful." I turned onto the street and parked in front of a dumpster that looked like it hadn't been emptied in a few years. It was in a slight alcove so it got the van out of the street.

"You have your gun?" Savage asked.

"It's under my coat." Which I'd been wearing since we left the agency. I figured the more layers between me and Savage, the better. Just for precaution's sake. But I was sweating like a fat kid in a candy shop, and there was no way I was taking my coat off now. There was a swamp in the layers between my skin and the down feathers.

I unbuckled my seatbelt and opened the car door, and then I started gagging at whatever horrific smell was leaking from the dumpster. It didn't even matter that it was so cold I was afraid I was going to break. I grabbed hold of the rearview mirror to steady myself.

"You okay?" Savage asked. "You don't look so good."

"Good God," I said, gagging again. "Don't you smell that?"

"Breathe through your mouth, not your nose," he said. "And please stop making that sound. A yeti is going to think you're trying to mate with it."

I gagged again in response and Savage sighed and took me by the elbow, leading me farther away from the dumpster.

"Sorry about that," I said. My eyes were watering so bad I could barely see what was in front of me until we were standing in the middle of the street right in front of the building Matthew Martin had disappeared into. I wiped my eyes and realized Savage had taken out his gun, holding it down at his side. Then he moved in a slow circle.

"What are you doing?" I asked, perplexed.

"Just letting all our new friends know that I expect the van to be in the same condition we left it in when we return."

"What friends?" But I started looking a little closer in the shadows and could see movement. We were surrounded by the scourge of the street. And then they scurried off in other directions like rats. "Oh, my," I whispered under my breath, suddenly very grateful for Savage's company. The garbage had distracted me, and I'd taken my eye off the ball.

"Maybe it's a brothel," I said.

Savage stared at me. "Yeah, with pet-sitting services."

"Maybe it's a different kind of brothel."

He shook his head and pointed up to the fire escapes above us. "You think you can get up there? The windows on the third floor aren't boarded up."

"Sure thing," I said, but I wasn't feeling overly confident. My mind wasn't in the game today, and all I really wanted to do was go back to the office and take a nap on my floor.

We were standing in front of the building next to the dog brothel, and Savage went over and pulled down the ladder from the fire escape. I cringed at the noise and looked around, expecting Matt Martin and his bulldog to run out of the building next door half-naked.

I sighed, seeing no other way around getting this job done, and went to the ladder, climbing up with all the grace of someone wearing a puffy winter coat and a sidearm. I waited for Savage to climb up behind me and pull down the next ladder. I wasn't quite tall enough, even when I jumped.

By the time we made it to the third floor I was both out of breath and freezing, and I could smell the occasional whiff from the dumpster. I gagged one more time for good measure, and Savage took a step back.

"I'm good," I said, and moved closer to the window to see if I could see inside. It was filthy and covered in grime, and some of the panes were broken out. "Do you hear that?"

Savage moved closer and the music swelled from inside. The bass thumped loud enough to rattle the windows.

"Perfect," Savage said, and reached inside the empty pane to push open the window.

"You can't do that," I hissed. "It's illegal."

He just stared at me. "Do you want to find out what Matt Martin is up to or not?"

"I left my camera in the van."

"Use your phone," he said, and then crawled through the window.

I felt like I was having an out-of-body experience. The wedding stress was making me feel like an idiot. And act like one.

I crawled through the window behind Savage and my coat snagged on something sharp. I heard the rip of fabric, and I swore under my breath. The floor creaked below me, and the smell of dust and must was overwhelming. Old wooden crates were piled high, and a wrong move could send them all tumbling down.

The third floor of the building was more of a loft. The entire middle area was open and looked all the way down to the first floor. That's where the lights and music were coming from, so we made our way closer to the edge.

I grabbed Savage's hand, not sure if I wanted to see what was going on below. I wasn't mentally prepared for a dog owner and canine brothel. Savage squeezed my hand and led me toward the edge anyway. The wooden floor was precarious at best and creaked noisily, and part of the railing was gone that looked down over the middle.

We squatted down and gingerly peeked over the edge. And then I burst into tears and fell back on my butt.

"What?" Savaged mouthed, looking at me with concern.

"It's a dog circus," I said between sobs. "That's the cutest thing I've ever seen."

Chapter Four

It was after noon once I dropped Savage back off at the agency. He'd been unusually silent on the way back, and he'd barely waved goodbye when he jumped out of the van.

I nixed my plan of taking a nap in my office because I'd have to explain why my face was red and swollen from crying and why there was a giant rip in my favorite coat. I decided the best thing to do was regroup, so I headed to Nick's house. I guess technically it was about to become our house, but I hadn't gotten used to saying that yet. I'd grown up in a tiny, three-bedroom, one-bath house and from the moment I'd graduated from college I'd been on my own to provide for myself. So it still felt weird to me to walk into Nick's house and think of it as mine, though he'd told me over and over again we could change whatever needed to be changed so I could put my stamp on it too.

It was just so…big. And out of my league. I didn't belong with the Nina Dempseys of the world, giving garden parties and wearing pearls to breakfast. I didn't have the lineage of the Savannah elite behind my name. I had bootleggers and crazy people in my lineage.

Nick's house was halfway between Savannah and Whiskey Bayou on a private road, secluded from the highway and the rest of the world. I turned into the long driveway and typed the code in to open the gate, and then drove on autopilot until I was parked in the driveway. Nick's car was gone, and I wondered if he'd managed to get any sleep. And then I wondered how many of our days and nights would be like this for the rest of our lives, waiting for him to come home after working days at a time and not knowing what was going on. It had put a heck of a strain on my parents' marriage, but I liked to think of myself as more evolved and understanding. After all, I had a busy career and life outside of Nick to keep me occupied while I was worrying about him.

I was so tired I could barely get my key in the door to unlock it, and once I did I just dropped my bag, coat, and keys on the hall table and dragged myself upstairs. I stripped out of my clothes along the way and got in a hot shower to warm my bones. I thanked God for the tankless water heater and might have fallen asleep standing up.

It was a good thing I'd snagged Nick because there were probably plenty of women who wanted to marry him for his bathroom alone. It had heated floors and towel rods, a walk-in shower with multiple pulsating shower heads, and a whirlpool tub that fit two people comfortably.

When I was warm and pruney I got out, wrapped myself in a fluffy towel, and then headed into the bedroom. Nick's side of the bed was still rumpled from where he'd napped. I crawled under the covers and was out almost before my head hit the pillow.

Something tickled my cheek and I swatted at it before slowly opening my eyes. Nick came into focus. He looked terrible. He was always handsome, it was just in his bones, but there were dark circles under his eyes and an exhaustion there that even sleep couldn't cure.

"What are you doing here?" I said, placing my hand on the side of his face and leaning in for a kiss.

"Looking for you. Rosemarie thought you might be dead in a gutter somewhere because you haven't answered your phone and you didn't go pick up Scarlet like you'd told her you would. She says she hopes you don't mind, but she might push Scarlet out of the car and into oncoming traffic."

I winced. I'd completely forgotten about Scarlet. "I left my phone downstairs on the table. What time is it?"

"After three."

I winced again and pushed back the covers.

"You must've had an exciting morning," Nick said, crawling into bed beside me and pulling me close.

"Pastor Charles came to my office and we made a trade so we could use the church for the wedding. Someone's messing with him, so I told him I'd investigate as long as we can have booze at the reception."

"Good thinking," Nick said, kissing me on the forehead. "We're going to need it."

"Then Kate ambushed me and brought my family and Rosemarie into the agency to start planning the wedding. My mom got drunk and Rosemarie ate all the cinnamon rolls. Aunt Scarlet hired me to find out if Savage has a micro-penis so she's not getting damaged goods when she makes her move. And then I went to a dog circus."

Nick seemed slightly stunned and just stared at me. "Normally I'd say that you were making all that up, but I know you too well. No wonder you're tired."

"Sorry you had to stop working to check up on me."

"No worries. I missed you. And I'm having to cut through a lot of red tape, which takes time. I put a call in to my grandfather."

"Always helps to have a senator apply a little pressure."

"You have no idea," he said. "But while I'm here, maybe we can take another nap."

He rolled me to my back and kissed me hard, and then I remembered that I'd only been wearing a towel when I got into bed. And then somehow Nick was naked and my troubles of the day disappeared.

Neither of us had time to linger, so we grabbed a quick shower, dressed, and went down to the kitchen for something to eat. All I'd had that day was a cinnamon roll and frozen trail mix. I wasn't sure when Nick had last eaten.

I made us peanut butter and banana sandwiches and drizzled honey over the top of both of them, and we ate them standing in the kitchen.

"I've got to go," Nick said, checking his phone. "I've got to meet with the mayor."

"That doesn't sound good."

"That's because we've put a halt to the merger for the time being while the investigation is going on. The company is making harassment noises and basically making everyone's life a living hell. And of course they're on personal terms with the mayor, so he's going to make my life a living hell."

"What are you going to do?" I asked.

"Hopefully arrest someone for murder soon. I'm making people uncomfortable. That's a good thing."

He kissed me goodbye and then was out the door. I threw away our trash and then went to find my other jacket. It was the South, so it's not like I had a variety of coats heavy enough to protect me from this kind of cold. But I did have a ski jacket from my one and only skiing experience. I'm not sure why I'd kept it. Maybe because it had been so expensive. Or maybe as a reminder that I should never get on skis again.

I dug to the back of the closet and pulled out a royal-blue ski jacket with a fur collar. And then I went back upstairs to change my handbag and get another scarf, hat, and gloves, because not matching was against every Southern woman's sense of decorum.

The good thing about black was it went with everything. So I grabbed a new Kate Spade tote, because having multiples of something you like is important, and the new hat, gloves, and scarf, and I headed back out to the van. I was feeling refreshed, and not nearly as insane as I had earlier. The wedding hormones were under control.

I had a little time before I had to be back in the city for the dress fitting, so I headed to Whiskey Bayou to see what I could find out about Pastor Charles's mystery stalker. The road was mostly deserted leading into town.

The best way to describe Whiskey Bayou was quaint southern charm with a touch of the apocalyptic. The bayous ran parallel down each side of the highway and surround the town, and big trees with moss made a small cocoon. The population had been at around three thousand people since I was a kid, so growth wasn't really happening like over at Tybee Island where developers were swooping in to put in luxury condos.

Whiskey Bayou had gotten its name because it had been a whiskey-making town long before the distillery was built. They were making whiskey all the way back to Revolutionary times and hiding it in the bayous so it wouldn't get taxed. And when prohibition hit in the twenties, Whiskey Bayou boomed because it was the only place to get booze in a hundred miles. There was even a speakeasy that people from the city would come for.

I took the access road off the highway and passed the old railroad graveyard to my left. It was like stepping back in time. The cars parked along Main Street were old, the buildings shabby with age. Mom and Pop shops filled the buildings, and The Good Luck Café sat on the corner. Just past the café was the park and the old whiskey distillery building, which had sat abandoned for almost thirty years, but had such sentimental value to the town no one wanted to get rid of it, and no one could afford to reopen it and use it.

I circled around the distillery and made my way back to the Good Luck Café. Most of the parking spaces down Main Street were empty because of the cold weather, so I didn't feel so bad when the van took up almost two. I still hadn't quite figured out how to park the thing yet.

The Good Luck Café had been an institution in Whiskey Bayou since the fifties. Not much had changed since then. The floors were black and white squares, and the tables were white Formica with turquoise chairs. There were a few booths along the back with the same turquoise vinyl seats.

There was a long countertop with red barstools, and three glass cake stands stood in a row with the different pies that had been baked fresh that morning. The heat was working overtime to stay up with the cold, and it was making an awful lot of noise through the vents. I looked around, but there were no customers in at the moment.

I took a seat at the counter and waited, knowing Jolene Meader had ears like a bat and would be out to check on me in a second. It took less than that for her to swing through the kitchen door and look me over.

"Well, Addison Holmes," she said, her Georgia accent thick. "Aren't you looking like the city now. All spit and polish. What brings you back home? Saw in the paper you were getting married, but it didn't say where."

I decided not to bring up the fact that Savannah was a fifteen-minute drive, and that I was home almost every weekend for horrible pot roast, or whatever else my mother was experimenting on in the kitchen. She was a great mom, but she'd never gotten the hang of cooking.

"At the church," I told her, smiling.

"Ah, a familiar stomping ground. I remember your first."

She was making it a challenge to keep a smile on my face. Jolene Meader had inherited the café from her parents. She'd been born to them late in life, and they'd called her their good luck baby, so that's what they named their café. Her parents had been sweet people, but had passed on when I'd been just a kid. Jolene baked like an angel, but she was mean as the devil. It was an odd combination, and one that had customers coming back for more abuse on a consistent basis. She'd never married or had children, so who knew what would happen to the restaurant when she was tired of it.

"I'll take a coffee and a piece of that peach pie," I said.

Jolene was somewhere in her mid-sixties, but she was holding up well. She was thin as a rail, probably from bussing tables for the last forty-five years, and her hair had been a bright shock of red for as long as I could remember. She never wore any makeup except for the bright red lipstick she kept in her apron pocket.

"Business been slow?" I asked.

"No one wants to get out in this cold. Makes the bones hurt. Even my pie isn't worth that."

I bit into a piece of peach pie and disagreed wholeheartedly. I would have walked across fire for that pie, and it was everything I could do to keep from licking the plate.

"I've got a client who's being bothered by a stranger in town," I said. "Takes pictures of him all over the place and then sends them to him. You seen any strangers around?"

She looked at me a few seconds and then said, "You want any more pie?"

What I should have said was no, but I opened my mouth and said, "Sure, one more piece won't hurt. I probably won't get to eat dinner."

"Not many strangers around town this time of year," she said. "Had a couple in the other day that took the wrong turn on their way to Tybee Island. But not surprising since I don't think they had a whole brain between them. Saw your aunt come through town the other day. Wouldn't put it past her to send creepy pictures to someone."

I pursed my lips and decided to take a sip of coffee. It's not like Jolene was *wrong*.

"She's retired," I said.

"Woman like that never retires. But I sure wish she'd do something with that whiskey distillery. Make it into a museum or something. Lord knows she's got more money than Midas."

"What?" I asked. "What distillery?"

Jolene looked at me like I had the IQ of a garden gnome. "Our distillery. She got it after her husband died. The third one, I think. She always made out like a bandit in her marriages. Smart woman, that Scarlet."

"I had no idea," I said.

"I remember Scarlet when I was a kid. She was kind of like the Bogeyman, no one would say her name above a whisper. She worked for the government a long time. Of course, no one was completely sure *which* government she was working for. Could've been all of them."

I wanted to ask more questions about Scarlet, but that wasn't the reason I was there. "No one else other than Scarlet and the other couple?"

"Not in the last few weeks. Just the regulars. Back before Thanksgiving I had a fella come in. Older gentleman, maybe in his fifties. Dressed nice. Expensive watch and bag. But you could tell he had some rough edges. Gave me the willies. Had dead eyes. I gave Sheriff Rafferty free pie just so he'd stay in the café while he was here."

"Anything stand out about him other than the dead eyes?" I asked. Some of the pictures of Pastor Charles were taken in the fall, so it was possible this could be the guy.

"Not really. Don't remember much else about him other than the eyes. They were brown. He paid cash. Didn't speak to no one other than making his order."

"He have an accent? Did it sound like he was from around here?"

Jolene thought about it for a second. "Nope, now that you mention it. No accent, but he definitely wasn't from around here."

"You see what he was driving?" I asked.

"Nope, he must've parked around back. Never saw him again after that so figured he was just passing through."

The café still used handwritten tickets, so she totaled me up and put the bill under my coffee cup. I grabbed cash out of my bag and decided not to complain that she'd charged me for four pieces of pie.

"Are you having an open bar?" she asked. "It'd be wrong to issue an open invitation like that and then only offer a cash bar."

I nodded noncommittally and got out as fast as I could.

Chapter Five

I STILL HAD a little time before I needed to head back into the city for the dress fitting, so I drove by the church in hopes that I could catch Pastor Charles again. There were no cars in the parking lot, and his car wasn't in the spot next to the rectory.

I pulled into the lot and got out his file so I could give him a call, and I went ahead and saved his number in my phone because I was sure I'd have to call him again about the wedding.

The phone rang several times before he picked up.

"Pastor Charles," he said.

"This is Addison Holmes," I said. "I'm in Whiskey Bayou checking out a couple of things for your case. Jolene Meador said she remembers seeing a man come in last November. White guy, dressed in new clothes with an expensive watch and bag. She said he looked rough though.

Brown eyes that creeped her out. Does someone fitting that description sound familiar at all to you?"

He was silent for several seconds, to the point I wondered if he was still on the line.

"No," he said. "That doesn't sound familiar."

"Would you mind if I had access to any personnel files at the church or any complaints that have been made? Maybe your secretary intercepted someone before they could complain directly to you."

"That's a good idea," he said. "Today is Beverly's day off, but I had her transfer everything to electronic files when I came to the church. I'll text her and let her know to give you anything you need. Just give her a call."

"I appreciate it," I said. "I'll be back in touch." I was about to hang up when I thought about the wedding. "Umm…do you need to meet with me and Nick before the ceremony on Friday?"

"Do I need to?" he asked, sounding surprised. "Is there a problem?"

"No, of course not," I rushed to say.

"Then we're good," he said. "I've had lots of practice. And you've had practice before too. All's good." And then he disconnected.

"Well," I said, looking at my phone. And then it rang again, but it was my mother.

"Addison," she said. She sounded like she'd been swallowing shards of glass. "I heard you were parked over at the church. Are you meeting with Pastor Charles about the wedding? Do you need me to come up there?"

I'd been in Savannah too long. I'd forgotten how fast the WB network worked. I looked around to see if anyone was watching me, but I couldn't see a soul. I grabbed my binoculars from my bag and looked down toward the Good Luck Café. Sure enough, there was Jolene standing at the window watching the van.

"I'm good," I said. "I'm actually here on business and just needed a place to pull over. You sound terrible. I thought you'd be out the rest of the day."

"Vince gave me his hangover cure," she rasped. "I have no choice but to be awake."

"Did it work?"

"I stopped throwing up. But it feels like I swallowed a sheep."

"Huh," I said. "That's different."

"That woman drives me to distraction," she said. "If this wasn't your wedding I'd run over her with a dump truck. Should've done it years ago, but now that your father isn't around to protect her I don't have any restrictions."

"You'd go to jail. Vince would miss you."

"They allow conjugal visits. I think it'd be worth it."

I squenched my nose up in disgust. That was more information than I needed to know.

"What's this about shady characters in town?" she asked. "Is someone making trouble?"

"Could be," I hedged. "You notice any strangers around the last few months?"

"Edith Gobel's nephew," she said. "He's come to visit a few times, and every time he does, things go missing out of her house. Rides a motorcycle, so it's probably why he's had to make so many trips to visit."

"What about strangers?"

"I don't go into town as often as I used to. Since Vince is retired we can go have our fun during the week, and then be back for church on the weekend. He took me to the casino in Mississippi last week. I won three hundred dollars on the penny slots."

I blew out a breath. There was no point trying to get information out of my mom the quick way. She wasn't capable of giving a short version of anything. But her mention of the church reminded me of something.

"You don't happen to know Beverly Jennings's home number, do you? I need to get some information from her."

"That's right, she's off on Mondays," my mother said. "I've got it here stored in my phone. I'll text it to you. What kind of information?"

"For the wedding," I lied. "I've got to go. Talk to you soon."

I hung up before she could start asking more questions. My lies would only get me so far. Phyllis Holmes was a master at ferreting out information from people. Aunt Scarlet should have hired her to find out information about Savage.

My mom was true to her word and texted me Beverly Jennings's phone number and I gave her a call, keeping an eye on the clock.

"Hello?" she answered.

"Mrs. Jennings?" I asked. "This is Addison Holmes."

"Oh, yes," she said. "Pastor Charles just told me you'd be reaching out. He said you were helping him with a private matter."

She sounded a little bit perturbed that he wasn't coming to her for help.

"Yes, I appreciate your help. I need to get a copy of all the personnel files for anyone who has worked at the church in the last ten years."

"That's easy enough," she said. "I can email them to you since they're all digitized now. I don't know why we had to change it from the old way. There's nothing like pen and paper, I always say. That's how records stay confidential. Now you put them in a cloud and everyone knows all your business."

"How long have you been secretary for the church?" I asked, curiously. I knew she'd been there when I was growing up.

"Thirty-four years. I've been through five pastors that have come and gone."

"I imagine you've gotten to be a pretty good gatekeeper," I said.

"You have to be," she said. I could practically hear her head nodding on the other end of the line. "The pastor has an important job to do, but he can't be everything to everyone in the congregation. He's got to delegate. That's why we have elders and deacons and volunteers. Everybody comes to me wanting to speak with the pastor, but it's my job to find out what's going on and gently persuade them that someone else is better suited to help them with what they need."

"Ever have anyone who doesn't want to be persuaded?"

"Oh, sure," she said. "I've had some doozies over the years. But nothing I couldn't handle. I'm tougher than I look."

That was a terrifying thought, because Beverly Jennings looked like a linebacker. She was the perfect person to run interference for the pastor.

"Anyone bother Pastor Charles that ever worried you? Or made you worried for him?"

"No," she said immediately. "Nothing like that. Do you think Pastor Charles is in danger?"

I wasn't sure how much to tell her, or how much Pastor Charles *wanted* me to tell her. But she was a sharp lady and had her pulse on everything going on with the church. And I was sure in her position she had to keep certain confidences.

"I think it wouldn't hurt to keep an eye on him and his

schedule. Make sure you know where he's going and who he's going to see."

She was silent for several seconds. "I see. I'll make sure to get you all the personnel files immediately. Anything else you need?"

"Just a list of anyone who's maybe been overzealous in getting close to the pastor. Maybe even a woman who's been overly interested or won't take no for an answer."

Beverly snorted out a laugh. "Lord, there's been plenty of those. I didn't even think of that. Pastor Charles is a good-looking man, and still in the prime of his life. Donna Larkin would be at the top of that list."

I winced sympathetically. Donna Larkin was a bulldozer. There wasn't anything she didn't get if she set her mind to it. It was probably driving her crazy that Pastor Charles had rejected her advances.

I thanked Beverly again for her help, and gave her all my information. And then I told her to call me day or night if anything unusual happened or she felt like something was off with Pastor Charles.

I hung up the phone no farther to where I'd started. It was hard to hide in a town the size of Whiskey Bayou. Even if you tried to skulk about and take pictures without anyone noticing, someone would have seen a vehicle or noticed something out of place. It was no wonder Scarlet had made such a great spy. Everyone in Whiskey Bayou was trained to snoop from the cradle.

Chapter Six

BY THE TIME I headed back into Savannah it was starting to get dark. It was also starting to drizzle.

Anyone who's from the south knows this is a terrible thing to happen. Nothing could stir panic in the hearts of Southerners like ice on the roads. Or ice anywhere, really. We weren't equipped to deal with it. We didn't have snow tires, extra blankets in our cars, or kitty litter in the trunk. We just gripped the wheel as tight as possible and screamed as we slid across the highway. I was grateful Nick wasn't working traffic.

By the time I got into the heart of historic Savannah, there was already a thin layer of ice on the roads and the sand trucks were out. From the looks of things, I'd be sleeping at the office tonight.

I found street parking easily when I got to Le Couture, mostly because no one else was insane enough to try wedding dresses on in an ice storm.

I'd barely turned off the ignition when Rosemarie ran out the front of the bridal shop. It took me a minute for my eyes to adjust because she was swathed in hot-pink satin, and it was hiked up to her knees so it didn't drag on the ground.

"Are you going to prom in 1988?" I asked. "Are we having a theme wedding?"

"Hurry," she said, skidding to a halt on the sidewalk. "It's a good thing you're early. They're going to close soon on account of the weather. There's dresses flying everywhere in there, and everyone is naked. I think I've lost three pounds since we started. I'm sweating like a pig."

"Not good for satin," I said.

She was holding the door open for me. Le Couture kept the front door locked, and only people with appointments were buzzed inside. The downstairs was just a small reception area with a sleek black counter, three black leather chairs, and a door that led back into an employees-only area.

I followed Rosemarie up white carpeted stairs to the second level and gasped at all the gowns. This was nothing like the first time, when I'd bought a wedding dress at the Bridal Barn. These were *dresses*. There were mirrors and a little stage area to twirl in. And racks of white dresses on one side and evening gowns on the other side for the wedding party.

There was a seating area, almost like a gallery for people to watch the spectacle, and sitting at opposite ends of the U-shaped black leather couch were Aunt Scarlet and Nina Dempsey.

It had been a while since I'd seen Nina. Actually, we'd only ever met once, and it wasn't on the best of terms since her husband tried to hit on me. She was dressed in a stiff navy winter suit with an ice blue shell, and she wore the pearls she never seemed to leave home without. I wondered if she slept in them.

Aunt Scarlet faced her, not blinking, and she'd undressed down to a hot-pink bra and panties. I'd spent a week with Scarlet at a nudist colony, so I figured Nina was probably in shock. Age and gravity hadn't been kind to Scarlet, despite the fact she'd had the occasional nip, tuck, lift, and implant through the years. She mostly looked like a sack of potatoes wrapped in liver-spotted skin.

They each held a glass of champagne.

Kate was standing behind them in a lovely powder-blue gown that gathered at one shoulder. She was holding up a bottle of champagne and an already full glass. "I think you're going to need this."

I didn't argue. I just took the glass and drained it. And then I directed my next words to Kate.

"This is supposed to be a simple wedding for close friends and family only. I want simple. Simple dress, simple everything. I just want to get married."

"You should have thought of that before you put an open invitation in the newspaper, young lady," Nina said. "The church only holds four hundred people. And of course, those are all *your* people. I had to send invitations by courier so Nick's side of the family would even know there was a wedding at all. Disgraceful."

"Oh, put a cork in it, Nina," Scarlet said. "You did no such thing. I'm good friends with your father-in-law and he said you sent out a mass email. Have another glass of champagne. Your son is damned lucky to marry my grand-niece. She's a resourceful girl, and your son better treat her right or he might find himself dangling off a balcony like my husband."

"Ridiculous," Nina said. "Everyone knows Albert died choking on a piece of bread. He probably did it on purpose after being married to you."

Scarlet gasped, and Kate shifted her weight slightly. I was wondering if she was planning to knock both of their heads together.

"You bitch," Scarlet said. "For your information, I was talking about Francesco. He was Italian. Very passionate. Fighting and making love. It was all the same. But you wouldn't know about passion. It's hard to do anything with a block of ice."

This time it was Nina's turn to gasp, and she came to her feet, clutching her pearls. Scarlet hopped up from her chair, mad as a hornet—all five feet of her—the extensions in her ponytail making her head fall back on her shoulders.

"I get the feeling y'all have known each other a while," Rosemarie said from behind me.

I'd completely forgotten about Rosemarie. She'd gone back into the changing room, and gone was the hot-pink satin prom dress and in its place was a canary-yellow toga of the same material. She looked like a shiny banana.

"Oh, sure," Scarlet said, waving the hand with the champagne glass in it so some splashed over the top. "That dress is terrible, by the way, Rosie. You look like one of those Day-Glo condoms. Me and Nina go way back. Had relations with her daddy back in the sixties." She shrugged. "I regret that one. It was the 'shrooms. She gets the ice block routine honest is all I can say."

Nina was red in the face and cocking her hand back to punch Scarlet when there was a *zzzzz* sound, and both of them dropped to the ground. Kate stood behind them unapologetically with two stun guns.

"I brought two just in case," she said.

"Good call," I told her. "You think Scarlet's too old for that?"

"Nah," Kate said. "She's breathing. Let's move them out of the way, so we can get finished with this."

"You must've had a hell of a day in court," I said.

"Don't ask," Kate answered.

The sales girl made a squeak and we all turned to stare at her. She looked terrified.

"We apologize," Rosemarie said. "They'll both be splitting the cost of everything we purchase here. Do you have more champagne?"

Before I knew what was happening I was stripped down to my panties and standing on the little platform in front of the three floor-to-ceiling mirrors. The champagne had taken away my need for modesty, and the fact that I should be laying off things like cinnamon rolls, peach pie, and champagne.

"Damn, girl," Rosemarie said. "How many cinnamon rolls did you have this morning?"

"I will kill you," I told her, giving her my death stare. "I'm under a lot of stress. This is stress weight."

"My mom called today and said you had five pieces of pie at the Good Luck Café," Kate said.

"Since when do you talk to your mother?" I asked. "And I didn't have five pieces of pie. I had two pieces."

"There's a lot of defensiveness in your tone," Kate said. "Maybe it has something to do with the fact you were asking about mysterious people skulking about Whiskey Bayou."

"Can't I care about my community?" I asked, holding out my arms so the poor sales girl could measure me. "Wouldn't you want to know if unsavory characters were roaming the streets in your neighborhood?"

"Yes, which is why I live in a gated community," she said. "You're acting strange. You know I'm going to get to the bottom of it. You've never been able to keep anything from me."

"No one is keeping anything from you," I said, rolling my eyes. "I'm just trying to get married. Y'all are supposed to be helping me do that."

"You're right," Kate said. "But you'd better hurry up with the dress. I think I saw Scarlet move."

The sales girls rushed back in with several dresses slung over her arm, and she began hanging them from the pegs on the wall. Another girl rolled in a cart with bridesmaids' dresses on it and then ran back out again. I couldn't say I blamed her.

"What about Phoebe?" Kate asked. "Why isn't she a bridesmaid?"

"I asked her," I said, eyeing the first dress the girl brought. It had a lot of lace and beads. Not simple. I shook my head at her and pointed to the one in the middle. "That one." And then I turned back to Kate who had also had enough champagne to strip down to nothing.

"What'd she say?" Kate asked.

"She said I was giving her a bad vibe, so she was going to pass. I pretty much expected a response like that. It's similar to the one she gave me when I tried to get married the first time."

Rosemarie hiccupped. "And look how that turned out. She was right. Maybe she's got the sight. She seems like the type." And then she flushed red and looked back and forth between me and Kate. "Sorry," she said. "Champagne makes me very blunt. They should serve real drinks at places like this. This never happens with a Highball."

I think I'd prefer champagne Rosemarie over "real drink" Rosemarie. Real drink Rosemarie had a tendency to make inappropriate sexual advances to everyone she passed. She also tended to dress like Bondage Barbie. There were many sides to Rosemarie.

I stepped into the gown, not really paying attention to myself as the sales girl tugged it up around me and started zipping and pinning. She'd turned me away from the mirrors, which I was secretly glad about because I was almost positive thinking about eating more peach pie had expanded my waistline.

"Have you had any luck with caterers for the reception?" Kate asked.

I was assuming she was talking to Rosemarie because I knew absolutely nothing about what was going on with the wedding.

"The little Italian place on Second can do it," she said. "They're taking care of everything and will get in and set up early Friday morning. They'll have a buffet spread for two hundred people."

"A buffet?" a voice said from the corner. It was like nails on a chalkboard.

I looked up in horror to see Nick's mother roll to her hands and knees and slowly get up. She looked like the Bride of Frankenstein. Her hair looked like it'd been brushed with a hand mixer and her lipstick was smeared across her face.

"I'll not have it," she said. "This isn't a Golden Corral. It's the wedding of the grandson of a senator."

"And me," I added dryly, but she ignored me.

She held up her hands like she was seeing them for the first time, and then looked down at her mussed suit. "What happened to me?" Then she looked down at Scarlet, still prone on the floor.

"Ummm..." I said.

"She sucker-punched you," Rosemarie said with a straight face. "Surprised us all. You were just standing there and it came out of nowhere."

Nina looked down at Scarlet for a few more seconds and then kicked her in the side. The rest of us all gasped in sync.

"That woman's the devil," Nina said, and then she turned her laser beam eyes on me. "You've got some of that in you. If my son ends up shot or dangling from a balcony there is no corner of hell where I won't find you. Do I make myself clear?"

I nodded.

"Good," she said and then looked to the sales girl. "Grace, I don't need a new gown after all. Apparently, I should go to the Goodwill and find some overalls to go along with the buffet."

Nina made a grand exit and then everyone looked back over at Scarlet. She was starting to twitch.

"What do you think?" Grace asked, taking a step back from the little stage I was on.

I turned to look at myself in the mirror and gasped. The dress was beautiful. It was just a long column of soft white satin with a small train, but it was exactly what I wanted.

"I'll take it," I said. And then I looked down and saw the small tag pinned to the bottom hem of the dress. The dress cost more than I made in an entire year when I was teaching. I almost felt guilty for letting Nina and Aunt Scarlet pay for it, but when I thought about it, I figured it was kind of like getting hazard pay and I probably deserved it.

I twirled in front of the mirror a couple of times and let my mind replay the scene I'd just witnessed between Nina and Scarlet until something jogged my memory.

"Wait a second," I said, and turned to Rosemarie. "You said they can cater for two hundred people?"

"Yep," she said. "That's the limit. They're a family-owned restaurant and don't have a huge staff. They're closing down the restaurant just to do your wedding."

I didn't even bother to ask how much they were being paid to close down their restaurant on a Friday night.

"What are we going to do?" I asked. "Whoever put that stupid open invitation in the paper has made a mess of things. We might have a thousand people show up."

"Especially since word is spreading about the open bar. Your wedding might be a good time for that intervention TV show to make an appearance. I didn't realize there were so many booze hounds in Whiskey Bayou."

"We can print a retraction in the paper," Kate said. "Or maybe we can use the park. It's right across the street. We can get a couple of food and drink trucks and it can be like a street party for your wedding. Only none of them will get to see the actual wedding until you and Nick ride off for your honeymoon."

"That's a great idea except for the fact that it's two degrees outside," I said.

Kate shrugged. "Anyone will show up for free liquor."

"We're not paying for an open bar for the entire town. That's insane."

"A little cold isn't going to stop the biggest party of the year," she insisted. "Think of the long-term investment you're making. It's not just you anymore. You've got to think of Nick too. People are fickle. What if Nick decides to run for office one day and the only thing people remember about him is that he kicked them all out of his wedding after issuing an open invitation. The damage is already done. Use it to your advantage."

Kate threw me off guard. Did Nick want to run for a political office one day? He'd never mentioned it. And I'd never asked. I always thought of him as being a cop forever, but maybe he had goals and dreams bigger than he'd ever shared with me.

"I think I need to make a phone call," I said, and stepped off the platform to get my cell phone.

I moved into one of the private dressing areas and called Nick. I had no idea if he would be able to pick up or not, but it seemed like these were all decisions we should've been making together.

"Hey," he said when he answered.

"Oh, good," I said, spotting the little couch in the dressing room. "I didn't know if you'd be able to answer." I laid out flat because it was easier to do that than sit down in the dress.

"I'm sitting in the little waiting area downstairs. The weather's getting bad and I didn't want you to have to drive home."

"Oh," I said. And then I wanted to burst into tears because it was such a Nick thing to do. "Have you been waiting long?"

"Nah, I had a patrolman drop me off, though it took a while for the lady to buzz me in. Apparently, I'd just missed my mother. Thank God."

"Yeah, about that…" I said.

"Do I want to hear this?"

"Probably not, but this falls under the whole two becoming one thing, so if I have to suffer, so do you."

He laughed a little, and I could picture him settling into the chair and getting comfortable. Nick was a guy's guy. He'd grown up in wealth with every advantage, and he was movie star handsome, but everyone got along with Nick. As long as they were on the right side of the law.

"Would you mind so much if we just left everything and everyone we know and move somewhere else?"

"Sounds good to me," he said, sounding so exhausted and fed up it made my heart hurt. "We could buy a tiki hut bar on some island and sleep in a hammock. It's not like we need the money."

"Wow," I said. "I take it the case isn't going well. You've never entertained my fantasies before."

"Excuse me?" he asked.

"I mean outside the bedroom," I clarified.

"That's better," he said and sighed. "I'm just tired. These people are so dirty. I know they did it. But they're so smug they're never going to get caught because they can tie up things with lawyers and red tape. Sometimes I wonder if it's worth it. You put one away and fifty more criminals sprout up in their place."

"Of course it's worth it," I said. "Think of what it would be like without you. You'll get whoever's behind this because I know you. There's a family lying in the morgue right now who deserve justice, and you won't stop until they get it."

He sighed again. "Yeah. What happened with my mother?"

"She tried to punch Aunt Scarlet, so Kate tased them both."

He barked out a laugh and said, "Oh, I'm really glad I missed her. She was probably mad as a wet cat."

"We told her Scarlet sucker-punched her and knocked her out. She was more upset because we're having an Italian buffet for the wedding reception. She said she was going to wear overalls."

"Good God," he said. "I've never seen my mother in pants. Why are we talking on the phone instead of in person?"

"Because I'm wearing my wedding dress and you're not supposed to see me in it. Are you planning to run for office?"

"Not today, he said.

I guessed that was as good of an answer as any. "I was

actually calling to ask about the budget for this whole thing."

"Spend what you need to," he said. "You've got access to the accounts."

"No, you don't understand." And then I explained about the open invitation in the paper and how our wedding had turned into a street party for Whiskey Bayou, complete with food trucks.

"I guess it could be worse," he said. "The open invitation could've gone out in the *Savannah Morning News*. If all the excitement is over and you've bought a dress, let's go home. Spend what you need to. We're only doing this once."

I disconnected and realized I was crying. How'd I get so lucky?

Chapter Seven

TUESDAY

When I woke up the next morning Nick was already gone to work. I remember him kissing me on the cheek before he left and telling me to get more sleep.

There was a cup of coffee on the nightstand, and it was still warm, so I was guessing he hadn't left too long ago. Our bedroom was a big space with large picture windows that looked out into the trees. The morning sunlight was hazy coming through the gray clouds, but the freezing drizzle hadn't lasted long. Most of Savannah would be getting a late start this morning to let the sand and salt trucks clear areas, so I wasn't in a hurry to get out of bed and head to the office.

I turned on the TV to check the weather and traffic while I drank my coffee. And then I made the mistake of looking at my phone. I had texts from Kate, Rosemarie, and Scarlet asking for me to call them the second I woke up. I ignored all of them and reached for my bag, pulling out my case files and laptop.

Working from home was looking like a better option by the minute.

I booted up the computer and loaded up the pictures I'd taken the day before of Matthew Martin and his dog. I was assuming his wife would be ecstatic that her husband was involved with a dog circus and not another woman. I typed up my report and then emailed everything over to Lucy.

My stomach rumbled uncomfortably, and I looked over at my empty coffee cup, trying to remember how old the cream was in the refrigerator. It had been a while since I'd been to the grocery store. I'd mostly been living out of the van or my office since Nick had been called away.

I noticed an email from Beverly Jennings with an attachment and clicked on it. She'd sent me all the personnel files I'd asked for and they were all labeled by name and date. I noticed the one that said Charles Whidbey and clicked on it. It seemed like a good place to start. He might not have had any trouble here, but that didn't mean there couldn't have been issues he didn't remember from way in the past.

I read through his file quickly. There wasn't a whole lot of information there. He'd been a pastor for more than twenty years, and had been associate pastor at two churches prior to moving to Whiskey Bayou. His college and seminary information were included along with professional references. No personal references listed. Maybe he'd always been a loner.

I typed his social security number into our background check software to get some more personal information. He was born in1963 in St. Louis. Got a football scholarship to Nebraska. Went to seminary after graduation. Married shortly after.

"Hmm," I said. He certainly didn't have a wife now.

I read down a little farther and saw she'd been killed by a drunk driver several years after he'd taken his first job at a church in Kansas City.

"Oh, no," I whispered, starting to tear up. And he'd never found anyone else after she'd died. He'd loved her too much. *Still* loved her. "That's so sad. And beautiful."

I sniffled and kept reading. After he'd left Kansas City he went to a small church in Silver Springs, just outside of Omaha, Nebraska, and he was there another ten years before he came to Whiskey Bayou.

I looked at the list of professional references he gave and decided my best bet for finding out anything was the church secretary, Tilda Sweeney. Women tended to have long memories and they gave the greatest details. I didn't know if she was still the church secretary, but I called the number next to her name anyway.

It rang several times before a man picked up. His voice was gruff with a slight accent.

"Yes, I'm looking for Tilda Sweeney," I said. "Is she available?"

The man was silent for several seconds before answering. "Tilda doesn't live here anymore."

"Does she still work at the church?" I asked.

"No." And then he hung up.

"Alrighty then," I said. "Rude man."

I looked the church up online and wrote down the number they gave on the website. And then I looked at the staff directory. There was Tilda Sweeney's picture at the very bottom. She was an older lady with mousy brown hair pulled back from her face, and she wore oval glasses. She looked exactly like I'd expect someone named Tilda Sweeney to look like.

I was about to dial the church number when my stomach rumbled again and my skin went clammy. I tossed the covers off and ran to the bathroom, and then quickly got rid of the contents of my stomach. Since there wasn't all that much to get rid of it didn't last long, so I crawled over to the sink so I could splash cold water on my face and brush my teeth.

I fell back into bed and pulled the covers up to my chin. I was worn out. I'd had a crazy few weeks—first with catching the Romeo Bandit at the nudist colony with Aunt Scarlet and Rosemarie, and then almost getting my liver surgically removed and waking up in a bathtub of ice. I really hadn't taken the time to rest. And piling a wedding on top of everything only seemed to be making my body revolt. If I could make it through the week I'd have two weeks off in some tropical paradise for our honeymoon. I could hold out that long. Maybe.

I restacked my case files and grabbed my phone to make the call again, but it was then I saw a picture of Scarlet flash on the television screen and the phone fell out of my hand. It was a still shot of her in a convenience store a couple of weeks ago, swallowed up in her enormous fur coat and pointing a gun at a guy who was robbing the store. She'd actually shot the guy's ear off to save the day, but the picture didn't look good.

"In other news, the police are looking for Scarlet Holmes. They believe she can give them crucial information about the death of crime boss, Big Mo. Holmes and the victim were reported to have a personal relationship, and Holmes has been known to have a colorful past. She worked for the OSS and then CIA until her retirement. Several of her husbands were killed under mysterious circumstances. Her niece, Addison Holmes, is a private investigator for the McClean Detective Agency. If you know the location of this woman, police are asking you call the hotline number at the bottom of the screen."

"Ohmigosh," I said.

I picked up my phone and dialed Scarlet's number. She answered on the first ring.

"Where have you been?" she hissed. "I've been texting for hours."

"I've been sleeping. It's icy outside."

"Hogwash," she said. "The roads are fine. Have you watched the news?"

"I just saw it," I said. "Why are you avoiding the police? Just go in and talk with them and get this over with. They just want to ask you a few questions."

"That's just what they tell you," she said. "What am I, stupid? They get you in their clutches and then they pull out your teeth. It's just like the war."

I raised my brow at that. "They're not going to pull out your teeth. That's illegal. Just tell them you don't know anything and then play the old lady card. You'll be out of there in a few minutes."

"You sure don't know a lot, girl. They'd have eaten you for breakfast during my day. Just remember that it's always more fun to torture than to be tortured."

"Right," I said. "Good advice. Here's my good advice to you—hiding from the police is never a good idea."

"Oh, really? What about the Gestapo? Lots of people hid from them."

I sighed and rubbed at the headache brewing behind my eyes. "Fine," I said. "Where are you? At your hotel?"

"Hell, no. I'm on the move. I've got a new I.D. and a new look. No one will look twice at me. I need a ride. Can you come pick me up?"

The best thing I could do would be to take her to the police station, but she was just a little old lady, and she'd obviously been traumatized by something in her past. I couldn't just leave her there.

"Where are you?"

"Your mother's house," she said.

That was surprising. "She let you stay there?"

"She doesn't know I'm here. Phoebe told me last night that your mom and Vince left for his lake house before the weather started getting bad. It was real easy to break in. They don't even have a security system."

"One of the perks of living in a small town."

"Stupid if you ask me. There's criminals everywhere."

"Obviously," I said. "I'll be there in about an hour. Stay put."

"10-4," she said. "I'm going to take a nap. I've been up for hours. Bring me something for breakfast."

She hung up, and I shoved everything back into my bag. I'd call the church about Pastor Charles later. I grabbed my phone, got out of bed, and headed to the bathroom. I turned on the water to as hot as it would go and stripped down to nothing. Then my phone rang. It was Rosemarie.

"Good news," she said. "I talked to Gerald Mobley. He's in charge of parks and recreation. He thought it was a great idea to have a town wedding reception. I just have to sign a bunch of permits for the food trucks and alcohol. But since basically the whole town will be there everyone is mostly willing to let it pass if not all the t's are crossed and i's are dotted, if you get my drift."

"You bribed them with free alcohol?" I asked.

"Yep, and it worked like a charm. I need a favor," she said.

"Anything," I told her. As much work as she was doing on this wedding I would've given her my kidney if she needed it.

"Can you give me a ride? My car doesn't do so well on icy roads."

I think what she meant to say was that she didn't drive so well on icy roads. If she'd thought about what she'd said at all she would've realized that Black Betty wasn't exactly known for hugging the roads on tight curves.

"Sure," I said. "I've got to pick up Aunt Scarlet anyway, so I'll swing by your place."

"Great, and maybe we can swing by the cake place," she said. "I talked to the lady and she said she's actually got a wedding cancellation for Friday, but you have to use the designs the bride and groom already picked because she's already made the patterns. But you do get to choose the flavor. She's got little samples of the cakes you can try."

"That was my favorite part of almost getting married last time. I'll be there in an hour. I've still got to shower. And I have to get work done today. I'm never going to finish these cases before Friday."

"Not a problem. We're a great team. We'll have all those cases done before the end of the day."

I wondered if she actually believed that. I hung up and had one foot in the shower when phone rang again. I sighed and just took it into the shower with me. I propped it in the corner shelf.

"Are you in a car wash?" Savage asked.

"Shower."

"Thanks for the image," he said. "Ready to get to work today?"

"I don't need a babysitter," I said. "And I've got Rosemarie and Aunt Scarlet for the day, so the van is going to be a little full."

"You're right. Hate to miss it, but my calendar just filled up. I finished the background check and sent it to your email, and I've got some calls out about your priest. Something weird going on there. I'll give you a call when I've got something solid."

He hung up and I lathered my hair, grateful I'd whacked it all off. It was a heck of a lot easier to maintain. I was rinsing all the shampoo out when the phone rang again.

"Come on," I growled, but then felt guilty because it was Kate.

"Did you see the news this morning?" she asked. "If not, don't turn on the TV."

"I saw it," I said. "Good plug for the agency."

"We don't need a plug. We've got more business than we can handle. And now we have a bunch of looney tunes trying to hire you. I thought Lucy was going to toss a can of tear gas into the lobby and make a run for it. Anyway, what are you going to do about Scarlet?"

"Nothing much I can do. They only want to ask her a few questions. She's not under arrest. And she doesn't want to be found. She's a private kind of person."

"Uh huh," Kate said. "Especially when she shot that guy's ear off and tossed a Molotov cocktail into Big Mo's bedroom."

"No one can prove that," I said. "I've got to go. I'm getting a late start."

"Join the club. I'm still sitting in traffic. Don't come downtown if you don't have to."

"I've got to go taste cake later."

"That was my favorite part of your last wedding."

Chapter Eight

It was February, and my patience had run out with the weather. Winter gear was a pain to put on and take off, and there was no moving fast. I'd picked black leggings and a royal-blue turtleneck that mostly covered my butt. I'd picked it because it matched my jacket perfectly.

By the time I drove into Whiskey Bayou I was right at the hour mark. The roads had all been sanded, and there was more traffic on Main Street than when I'd been there the day before. Apparently, everyone had decided to show up for work today.

The house I'd grown up in was on the other side of town, past the fire station and the school. It was a little three-bedroom rock house with a shaker roof and diamond-paned windows. It was like a little fairytale cottage, and I'm sure it was adorable to anyone that didn't have to grow up in it with only one bathroom. One of the first things my mom had done after my dad had passed away was paint the front door bright magenta. My dad was more of a neutral kind of guy.

The second thing she did was sell her very practical beige Corolla and buy an exact replica of the General Lee from the Dukes of Hazzard. I shuddered to think of how much of her personality my mom has kept hidden over the majority of her life.

I pulled up in front of the house, and was going to get out to help Scarlet, but she must have been waiting by the front door because she was already closing it behind her before I could get out.

I hurried up the sidewalk to help her. She was weighed down with a floor-length mink coat and a duffle bag slung across her body. She was also dragging a suitcase behind her. Her ponytail was a little worse for the wear this morning, a few sprouts sticking out from the side of her head, but she'd taken the time to put on bright red lipstick.

"Good grief," I said. "Where'd all this stuff come from? I thought you left most of your stuff on the cruise ship."

"I'm switching cruise lines," she said. "They stopped serving all-you-can-eat crab legs in the lounge, and they hired a new girl to call out the bingo numbers. She mumbles. I would've had blackout if I could've heard the last number she'd called. She cost me a thousand bucks. It was the mega pot."

"Yikes," I said. "Bad for business." I put her bags in the back and then helped her into the front seat.

"You're telling me. All us life cruisers jumped ship at the next port. They lost business a lot sooner by cutting corners."

"Sooner than what?" I asked.

"We're all gonna die soon. All us life cruisers are at the end of the road. Someone's always dying on the ship, and they stick them in the little morgue way down at the bottom. I paid them a fortune so I could at die at sea, and look how they betrayed me. I told the captain straight to his face that I wouldn't have it."

I'd never understand Scarlet's fascination of dying on a cruise ship, but she said it had been a dream of hers for most of her life. I guess when you'd spent most of your life as a spy and dealing in life and death situations, you had a tendency to think about how you wanted to die.

"What'd you do with the rest of your stuff?" I asked.

"I rented a storage locker near the port," she said. "A car will pick me up Friday and drive me to Florida. The new ship departs Saturday morning."

"I'm getting married Friday," I said.

"Perfect timing," she said. "I hate weddings. And I went to your last one."

"But I didn't get married."

"It's all the same. Same people, same clothes, same food, same music..." She waved her hand in the air. "I'm heading to Australia. Y'all come visit me down under and I'll treat you to the best damned crab legs you've ever eaten. Where are we going first? I've got to stay incognito to avoid the Fuzz."

I blew out a breath and put the van in gear. "I've got to stop by and pick up Rosemarie. Her car doesn't handle icy roads well."

"Hmmph," Scarlet said. "That girl is a terrible driver on dry pavement."

I grunted in agreement, still a little perturbed about the wedding diss. Aunt Scarlet and I had been through a lot together. I was probably the closest family member she had.

By the time I'd pulled up to Rosemarie's little duplex, Aunt Scarlet had put on sunglasses and moved to the back seat.

"I'm too visible in the front," she said. "If you get pulled over I'm going to hide in the bathroom. I can probably kick the toilet out of the way and crawl out the bottom of this thing if push comes to shove."

"I'm sure it won't come to that," I said.

I texted Rosemarie to let her know we were there, and we waited as she stood at her open door and kissed her dogs goodbye like she was never going to see them again. She had two Great Danes that she'd named Johnny Castle and Baby, and her relationship with them was ambiguous at best.

"That's sad," Scarlet said. "Those dogs probably spend most of their time licking their butthole, and there she is kissing them like they've got gold bullion stuck in their teeth. You never know what people do in their personal lives. There's a lesson in that somewhere."

"What kind of lesson?" I asked. And then I mentally kicked myself.

"Never trust anyone. They might be secondhand butthole lickers and then where will you be?"

Rosemarie opened the passenger door and hoisted herself in. She was wearing her bright yellow puffy coat and a matching hat with a white puffy ball at the end. She had perpetually rosy cheeks and hair the color of corn silk that she wore feathered back from her face like Farrah Fawcett.

"Lord, it's cold out here," she said, little puffs of breath escaping her mouth. "Johnny Castle nipped my earlobe and I thought part of it snapped clean off."

I wrinkled my nose but didn't say anything, and then I took the long way through town so I could drive by the church and see if Pastor Charles was there or if anyone was lurking about. His car was there, a blue secondhand Toyota, and it was parked in front of the rectory. There were several other cars in the lot this morning as well. It reminded me that I still needed to call the church in Silver Springs, Nebraska and talk to Tilda Sweeney. I just added it to my mental list of tasks I still needed to get done for the day.

"Here," I said, handing Rosemarie my stack of case files. "Look through these on the way to the cake place and tell me which looks the easiest to get done. They weren't supposed to give me anything that involved too much prep work or recon, unless those last two cases Lucy gave me are doozies."

"Spy," Scarlet said.

"Excuse me?" I asked.

"That Asian vampire girl. She's a spy. I know my own kind when I see them. She's got a good cover. Secretary my ass."

Since those were some of the most sensible words I'd heard Scarlet speak recently, I thought it might be worth it to probe a little more.

"Who do you think she works for?" I asked.

"Looks like a spook to me," Scarlet said. "She's deadly, I know that for sure. Look at the way she moves. Always in a position where she can easily snap a neck or stab someone with one of those chopsticks she wears in her hair. If I was Kate I would watch my back. She's probably privy to some pretty secret information with the level of clients that agency draws."

"Interesting," I said.

"I think she's very nice," Rosemarie chimed in, looking back at Scarlet. "She's just a little shy. That's probably why she feels comfortable around me."

I almost slammed on the brakes. "I'm sorry, what?" I asked. "Are you saying you've spoken to her?"

"Sure," Rosemarie said, looking confused.

"Actual words?" I asked again.

"Sure. What else would she use to answer the phone all day? She's just very professional. But get her talking about things she's interested in and she'll talk your ear off."

"What's she interested in?" Scarlet asked, scooting up in her seat.

"Oh, you know," Rosemarie said, her hands animated. "The usual stuff. She likes puzzles."

I relaxed a bit. That didn't sound like the hobby of someone who killed on a daily basis.

"Oh, and she's a black belt in all kinds of stuff," Rosemarie continued. "And she likes knife throwing and is an expert marksman. And she said she's pretty good with a bow and arrow too. And parachuting. She's one of those extreme sportsmen. Jumps out of all kinds of planes and off waterfalls and stuff. And she occasionally paints."

"Paints?"

"You know," she said. "Like Picasso. She's a real Renaissance woman."

My eyes met Scarlet's in the rearview mirror and I raised my brows. She mouthed the word spy, and I had to agree.

Kate had been right about traffic heading into downtown Savannah. It was at a standstill for miles, and I was starting to get hungry. I was on less than empty after my bad coffee experience.

"I can't take this traffic much longer," Scarlet said. "I could walk faster. I've got to pee and I'm hungry."

"We're going to eat wedding cakes for lunch," Rosemarie said.

"I guess that'd be okay," Scarlet said. "I did a cake diet once. I lost a bunch of weight on account of all that icing makes you poop like a goose."

"Good to know," I said. I took Truman Parkway all the way to President Street, along with everyone else trying to get into downtown.

"You should've gotten off on Wheaton," Scarlet said. "The best cakes in Savannah are on Taylor Street."

"Oh, no," Rosemarie said, shaking her head. "The cake shop is on Drayton. These are the best cakes I've ever had. No one comes close to making cakes like Suzanne."

I decided to divert the conversation before Rosemarie and Aunt Scarlet got into a pissing match over cakes.

"Did you see anything interesting in the case files?" I asked Rosemarie.

"No, they all look boring. Nothing high-stakes like we're used to."

"What's wrong with them?" Scarlet asked. "They can't give us these kinds of cases. We're a BFD. We've got reputations to maintain."

"I figure it's a toss-up between the cheating wife and the fraud," Rosemarie said.

"Let's go with the fraud," Scarlet said. "After Big Mo, I've seen all the dong I want to see. In all my years, they've never gotten any better looking. You ever wonder why God made penises?"

"Nope," I said.

"All the time," Rosemarie said, nodding in agreement. "I have so many questions to ask God when I get to heaven, and that's one of them."

"I'll ask him for you," Scarlet said. "And then I'll send you a message with the answer. Unless you go first, then you can ask him yourself."

Rosemarie pressed her lips together, and put the other files back in my bag.

"I have to go to the bathroom," Scarlet said. "I'm an old lady. I can't hold it like I used to."

It took her several tries to get out of the seat because her hair and the fur coat were weighing her down. When she stood up she shrugged out of the mink so it fell to the floor and made her way back to the tiny bathroom. I caught a glimpse of her in the rearview mirror, and was glad I was stopped in traffic. She was wearing a skintight leopard print velour tracksuit and white sneakers, her ponytail bobbing as she made her way down the aisle.

"I'm never going to find parking," I said to Rosemarie. "I'll drop you and Scarlet off and see if I can find a miracle."

"There's no way this thing will fit in the parking garage," she said. "Maybe park in the alley. There's lots of service trucks in and out. Just put on your flashers and maybe they'll think you're making a delivery. It's not like we're going to be in the cake place that long."

She made a convincing argument. Traffic started moving again, and I heard a loud thump from the back along with the toilet flushing.

"You think she's okay?" I asked.

"Demons never die," she said, repeating my mother's sentiment. "It was everything I could do not to look for stray lightning when she said she was going to ask God about penises when she gets to heaven. That woman is probably on a first-name basis with Lucifer. Though maybe she knows both of them. She's been around since the beginning of time."

I grinned as we came up a side street near the bakery, and I made a turn into the narrow alleyway. It wasn't trash day, so I wasn't concerned about the garbage trucks being able to get in and out. The sign on the brick wall clearly said the alley was for delivery only. Since I was delivering all of us to the cake shop I thought Black Betty fit the parameters nicely.

Scarlet came stumbling out of the bathroom like she'd spent the last ten minutes in a martini shaker and she grabbed her mink off the ground.

"Y'all probably want to vacate the premises," she said. "I don't know what happened in there, but it wasn't pretty."

It smelled like an animal had died and been left out in the sun for three days. I started gagging, and I hit the flashers and jumped out of the car. I was sweating like a pig, and sucked in a deep breath, trying to keep the nausea down.

When I felt like I was halfway in control of my gag reflex I looked over at Rosemarie. She was pale, sweat dotted her upper lip, and her hat sat askew on her head.

"Maybe you should just abandon it," she said, panting. "Leave the keys in it and see if someone steals it."

"Whew," Scarlet said, wrapping her coat around her. "That cold air will take your breath away. Come on, girls. I made some room for some cake. I'm starving."

Rosemarie and I followed Scarlet out of the alley and Rosemarie whispered, "There's only one explanation for why no one has ever murdered that woman in her sleep."

"What's that?" I asked.

"She made a deal with the devil."

I hated to talk bad about family, but I was starting to think Rosemarie might be right.

Chapter Nine

"CRAZY CAKES?" I said, looking up at the flashing sign in front of the cake shop. "What the hell is Crazy Cakes?"

The display windows were eclectic to say the least. There was a naked mannequin wearing nothing but purple and gold Mardi Gras beads and holding a cake shaped like a very nice pair of breasts, complete with nipple and a thorny rose tattoo. There was another mannequin kneeling on top of a pile of gold doubloons holding a tray of cupcakes shaped like penises. There were even electric sparklers stuck in the end of each one to complete the look.

"She makes sex cakes?" I asked, completely stunned.

"She makes every kind of cake," Rosemarie said. "Look at this one." She pointed to the next display window.

It was a woodland scene with trees and a family of small bears, and cooking on a spit over a fire was a pair of squirrels that looked suspiciously like Chip and Dale. They were skewered and their eyes were open with little x's on them.

"Ohmigod," I said.

"Isn't she great?" Rosemarie asked. "She's taking Savannah by storm. We're so lucky there was a cancellation for Friday. Let's go in and taste some cake."

Rosemarie opened the door and a warm blast of air greeted us. The inside of these old buildings downtown mostly looked the same—original wooden floors and high ceilings with exposed beams and ductwork.

"Oh, wow," I said. My mouth started watering the second we stepped inside. It smelled heavenly.

"I think I just had an orgasm," Scarlet said. "I don't know what kind of cake that is but I want to make love to it."

"Suzanne sells cake batter in her erotic cake kit, along with the plastic sheets so you don't get your floor dirty."

"I don't understand," Scarlet said. "You bake an erotic cake on the floor?"

"No, you pour the batter out on the plastic sheet and make love on top of it. Food can be very sensual."

"Huh," Scarlet said. "I'll have to try that."

"Please, God," I whispered. "Make it stop."

There was a long glass case filled with pastries, pies, and cakes. It was the most beautiful thing I'd ever seen, and I wanted to buy everything.

"Y'all hold on a second," a voice from the back said. "I'll be right out."

"That sounds just like Kathleen Turner," Scarlet said. "Did she quit acting to open a cake shop?"

"It's us, Suzanne," Rosemarie called out. "We're here for the tasting."

"I'm just getting y'alls cake samples together," Suzanne called back. "Take a seat at the little table. Help yourself to coffee, tea, or water there on the credenza."

"You should get some of those penis cupcakes for the reception," Scarlet said. "I'd pay a thousand bucks to see Nina Dempsey eat one of those things."

"I thought you weren't going to be at the wedding?" I said.

"I've got eyes everywhere," Scarlet said. "Never forget that."

The kitchen door swung open and Suzanne came though pushing a tea cart. There could've been a million dollars or a naked Hugh Jackman on that tea cart. I wouldn't have known, because my eyes were glued to Suzanne.

"Holy shit," Scarlet whispered.

Suzanne was several inches over six feet and had the blackest, most flawless skin I'd ever seen. Her hair was platinum blonde and parted down the middle, her brows skillfully arched, and her contouring was at Kardashian level. She was wearing a red, skintight jumpsuit and four-inch platform boots in black. She also had an Adam's apple.

Rosemarie squealed and jumped up to hug Suzanne, and then she turned back to us, beaming.

"This is Suzanne," she said. "We went to college together."

"We both sang in the choir," Suzanne said. "And now look at us."

My brows raised of their own volition. Seeing Suzanne and Rosemarie standing side by side, it was kind of a shock to the eyes.

"How do you get your cleavage to look like that?" Scarlet asked.

"It's a little trade secret, but since you're about to eat my cake I'll let you in on it. You've got to use tape. Makes 'em stand up real perky, and gives you just the right amount of cleavage."

"What kind of tape?" she asked. "Duct tape? That stuff holds everything together. You can put a boat back together with it after you saw it in half."

"Why would you saw a boat in half?" Rosemarie asked.

"Why do you want cleavage?" I asked, and then decided I didn't really want to know the answer. "Don't use duct tape on your breasts." As thin as her skin was it would take everything off.

Scarlet wasn't done asking questions. "How do you walk in those shoes? Can you show me how to get my hair to do that? I just got these extensions, but they're a pain in the behind. Feels like I got little cockroaches clicking around on my scalp, and sometimes I'm just doing nothing and my head falls back because they're so heavy."

"Honey, that's why I always go with a wig," Suzanne said. "I can have different hair every day, and it's always beautiful."

"Oh," Scarlet said. "That's an even better idea. How do you keep it on your head? Say you get in a fight and someone snatches it. I get in the occasional fight from time to time."

"I hear ya, sister," Suzanne said. "Ain't nothing gonna stop a ho from tearing a wig off your head. Sometimes sacrifices have to be made."

"Ain't that the truth," Scarlet said. "Why do hos always go for the hair first?"

Scarlet, Rosemarie, and I were seated at a little round table in a nook, and Suzanne put five small plates in front of each of us and a glass of ice water.

"The water is to cleanse your palate between bites," she said.

My stomach growled audibly.

"You guys really lucked out that I had a cancellation," she said. "I was real upset about it too because I had to make the molds by hand for the groom's cake. I'm an artist inside and outside the kitchen. But people don't appreciate that. They think I just whip some batter together and make a cake. I've been working on these cake designs for three months."

"Wow," I said. "At this point we're happy to take whatever you can give us."

"Good," she said. "Because I don't have time for anything else. I've got two weddings and a baby shower Friday night. Y'all go ahead with the tasting and I'll go back and get the design boards. I can do any flavor you want except the tres leches. It's too soft for the design."

I barely waited for Suzanne to turn her back before I started shoving cake in my mouth. "Ohmigod," I mumbled. It melted on the tongue. Chocolate, lemon, hummingbird, vanilla, strawberry…every one of them as good as the one before.

"You think she'd come work on my cruise ship?" Scarlet asked. "People of the sea need this kind of cake."

"Everyone needs this kind of cake," Rosemarie said. She'd forgone the fork and was down to licking the plate.

Suzanne came back in with two tri-fold boards, and she looked down at all our empty plates.

"Damn," she said. "Did you actually taste any of it?"

"You make very good cakes," I said, and then hiccuped. "I want them all."

"We could do that," she said, and then opened the tri-fold board to show the bride's cake. It was five tiers, each cake separated by short columns, and then there were two additional tiers on each side, and an honest to goodness waterfall that was coming out of one of the side tiers.

"Holy moly," I said.

"From what I understand, you're having a large wedding, and this will be enough to feed everyone. The original owner of this cake was going to do vanilla for all the tiers, but if you want I can do a different flavor for each one, and I'll make you and your man miniature ones in your favorite flavors so you can take them with you as a snack. The bride and groom never get to eat."

"Yes," I said, more excited about that than I probably should have been. I didn't care if anyone came to the wedding. All I cared about was that cake. "Please marry us and live with us and make cakes forever."

Suzanne threw her head back and laughed, deep and throaty. "You'd be surprised how many offers I get like that, but Suzanne is just too damned expensive. I'm single and I like to mingle, and I'm very picky about my dingles, if you get my drift."

"I hear ya, girl," Scarlet said. "We were just talking about penises on the way over here. I'm going to ask God why he made them when I get to heaven. It just seems like there could've been a better design. They're ugly and they get in the way."

"I know mine does," Suzanne said, and Scarlet's mouth dropped open in surprise.

Rosemarie clapped her hand over Scarlet's mouth before she could ask any more questions and I lost out on a chance for great cake.

"What about the groom's cake?" I asked.

"Whew," she said. "This one's been a challenge, but as an artist I'm always looking for ways to learn and grow my talent. What does your husband do for a living?"

"He's a cop," I said.

Suzanne pursed her lips and her penciled eyebrows rose almost to her hairline. "I dated a cop once. Kinky bastard. They all are. I suppose you're aware of the divorce rate for cops."

"I'm aware," I said.

"Is your husband a hunter, by chance?" she asked. "Other than a hunter of people, I mean."

"Not that I'm aware of," I said.

"Hmm," Suzanne said, and then opened the tri-fold board to show the groom's cake.

"Holy mother…" Scarlet whispered.

Rosemarie crossed herself.

My brain hadn't yet caught up to what my eyes were seeing. I was almost positive it was a bison head, just like a hunter would stick on his wall.

"I've really perfected my technique," Suzanne said. "I can make the hair look real. You won't be able to tell the difference between the cake and the real thing by the time I'm through."

"That's what we're afraid of," Scarlet said.

"You think Nick will notice?" Rosemarie asked.

"Maybe he'll be so tired from the case that he won't remember," I said. "But just in case, let's make sure he doesn't see it until after we're married."

"Don't worry," Suzanne said. "People are going to love it. There are a lot of hunters in this area. And if you pick red velvet for the cake it'll look even more authentic when you cut into it."

I thought of Nick's family. "Uh huh," I said.

"This is going to go real good with Nina's overalls," Scarlet said, her grin a little bit evil. "I might just show up to this wedding after all. It's going to be a train wreck."

Chapter Ten

WE LEFT the cake shop just under an hour after we'd arrived, and Rosemarie had one more thing to check off in her growing binder.

When we made it back to the alley, I was surprised and relieved to see the van was just where I'd left it. The only difference was that Nick was leaning up against it.

"I drove by and saw a couple of patrolmen looking it over," he said. "Said they got calls about a bad odor."

"You don't want to know," I said, leaning in to kiss him. "We have cakes. How do you feel about bison?"

He cocked his head to the side, looking at me curiously. "I don't hate them."

"Good," I said. "Let's just stick with that."

He kissed me again. "Your lips taste really good." And then he kissed me once more, licking at my bottom lip a bit.

"It's the cake. I tried to get her to marry us so she'd make us cakes every day, but she's single and she likes to mingle."

"It's a shame," he said. "I've always fantasized about having two women, especially one who bakes cakes."

"Then the fact she has a penis would probably throw you off your game," I told him.

He jerked back at that, the fantasy clearly ruined.

"Suzanne is a dude, but she makes the best cakes you will ever put in your mouth."

He kissed me again, and little harder and longer this time, and I melted into him.

"I'd have to agree with that," he said, coming up for air, out of breath. "I really miss you."

"I miss you, too. What are you doing here?"

"I've got another meeting with the mayor. I might get fired."

"That usually means you're doing something right," I said. "Give him hell. I've got to get back to work. I've still got cases to wrap up before we can leave on the honeymoon. I want to make sure I've got nothing on my mind for the next two weeks but being naked and warm."

"Something we both agree on," he said. "Stay safe. I'll call when I can."

He kissed me one more time and walked out of the alley, and I turned to see Scarlet and Rosemarie.

"Glad to see you're all toasty warm," Scarlet said. "I'm freezing my bippy off. Open the damned doors."

"Sorry," I muttered, but couldn't help my grin. Nick sure knew how to kiss.

"All that cake made me hungry," Rosemarie said once we got in and I started the car. "Maybe we should drive through somewhere."

"I could eat," I said, and we found the nearest Chick-fi-let, mostly because it was the only drive-thru where I could fit the van under the clearance sign.

I placed our order and we were in and out with the kind of efficiency that only Chick-fi-let was capable of, and I pulled into a non-metered parking space next to one of the cemeteries so we could eat.

Now that wedding stuff had been taken care of, I needed to get my head back in the game for work. Most specifically, for Pastor Charles. Something had been bothering me ever since I'd called that number on the reference sheet that morning.

I looked in the rearview mirror and Scarlet and Rosemarie had pulled the little table down between the two seats so they could eat. They were engrossed in conversation, so I took advantage of the moment and put my earbuds in so I could make the call to the church.

It rang several times before a woman's voice answered. "Silver Springs United Methodist Church," she said. "How can I help you?"

"May I speak to Tilda Sweeney, please?" I asked.

"This is Tilda."

"My name is Addison Holmes, and I'm calling from Whiskey Bayou, Georgia about Pastor Charles Whidbey."

"Oh, of course," she said. "We heard the news. We miss Pastor Whidbey so much. He was such a kind man."

"I'm actually a private investigator working on a case. I was hoping you might be able to help me with my investigation. Do you remember if there were any congregation members who had issues with the pastor, or if there was ever any trouble from non-congregation members? Maybe even some women?"

"That makes sense," she said, and then she blew out an audible breath. "Everyone loved the pastor. And I can't think of a single problem we ever had, or a congregation member who got out of hand. Sure, there were women from time to time who'd want to meet with him privately or they'd stop by his home with home-cooked meals. But he'd never engage. He was young and handsome, after all. He was very firm about always leaving the door open and making sure everything was above board. He was a kind and gentle soul."

"If anything comes to mind, I'd appreciate it if you'd give me a call. The pastor's life could be in danger."

She was silent for several seconds. "Is that supposed to be some kind of joke?" she snapped. "It's not funny."

"No," I said, thoroughly confused. "Pastor Charles has been having problems with a stalker recently, and has received threats. I'm just following up to see if something from his past maybe followed him here."

"I don't know who you think you are, young lady, but Pastor Charles's body was found last fall. He was a good man who doesn't deserve whatever sick joke you're playing."

"Wait…" I said, but she'd hung up. I stared at the phone and then dragged out my laptop. "That certainly adds a twist to things."

I did a search for death certificates in the database, and sure enough, there was one for Charles Robert Whidbey, dated October second of last year. I read through all the personal information. The DOB and place of birth matched what was in Pastor Charles's personnel file.

"Caucasian," I said. "Six-foot-one and a hundred and sixty pounds. Green eyes and brown hair. No physical markings or characteristics on the body. Mother's maiden name was O' Sullivan. That's very Irish."

"Who you talking to, girl?" Aunt Scarlet asked from the back seat.

"Myself," I answered back and shoved another fry in my mouth.

"Crazy as a June bug," I heard Scarlet say, but I ignored her.

Nothing was adding up. The real Charles Whidbey was a tall, thin, Irishman. The Charles Whidbey that was sitting in his office at the church in Whiskey Bayou was short, stocky and swarthy.

Then I scanned the bottom of the page that listed cause of death. Blunt force trauma to the head, multiple broken ribs and other bones. He was beaten to death.

I called Savage and waited while the phone rang, but it went to voicemail. "Hey, it's me," I said. "Can you get me the coroner's report for the death of Charles Whidbey? I'm looking at his death certificate as we speak, and it looks like my client isn't exactly who he claims to be. No hurry. I'll be in the field for a little while."

I hung up and then called Beverly at the church, not having a clue what I was going to say.

"First United Methodist Church of Whiskey Bayou," she said cheerfully.

"Man, you guys need to get a shorter greeting," I said. "That's a mouthful."

"Tell me about it," she said. "Don't tell anyone, but sometimes I just say hello. Who is this?"

"Oh, sorry. It's Addison Holmes. Is Pastor Charles in? He's not answering his cell and I need to follow up on a couple of things."

"I haven't seen him today," she said. "His car is parked at the rectory, but he's not been to his office today. I went to check on him a little while ago to see if everything was okay because he missed a couple of appointments this morning. Sometimes he likes to go on long prayer walks and he'll lose track of the time."

"Okay," I said. "Would you just have him give me a call whenever he gets back?"

"Sure thing," she said.

"No unusual activity this morning?"

"Nope, same as usual. Everyone's real excited about the street party at your wedding. Where did you register? I've had several people ask."

"Oh," I said, going blank. I'd completely forgotten about registering. And it's not like we needed stuff anyway. We had a house and all the stuff that went in it. "Just tell everyone to make a donation to the church instead in lieu of gifts."

"Wow," she said. "That's very nice of you."

I mmhmmmed and said goodbye as quickly as I could. I didn't tell her they were probably going to need all the help they could get after it was discovered Pastor Charles was an imposter and he might have killed a man to take over his identity. Whatever the outcome, it was going to be a scandal for the church.

After we were finished eating I pulled out my file for Zoe Willis.

"I don't know about you guys," Scarlet said. "But I could use a nap. They must put that turkey tryptophan in their chicken. I have a little of that stuff and I'm out like a light. I can barely make it through the meal before falling asleep in my gravy."

"Or it could be that you ate five pieces of cake, a chocolate shake, chicken nuggets and a large fries," Rosemarie said. "Anyone would want a nap after that."

"That's why I always wear stretchy pants," she said. "Goes back to my days as a spy. You never know when you're going to have to scale the side of a building or make room for a little extra dessert. They're all-purpose pants."

"I don't wear anything else," Rosemarie said. "Nobody ain't got time for buttons anymore. It's a health hazard if you ask me. I sat down once and had a button pop right off. My pop had to wear an eyepatch for the rest of his life."

"Y'all put yourself together," I said. "We're about to go shopping."

"What for?" Scarlet asked. "I didn't bring my shopping shoes. I've got to dress for comfort when I go shopping. I can't be wearing my fancy duds. They make my feet hurt."

I looked down at her sensible white sneakers and wondered what her shopping shoes looked like.

"This is a different kind of shopping," I said. "We're shopping for a criminal."

"I'm good at shopping for those," Scarlet said. "Who are we killing today?"

I pinched my lips together and shook my head. "No one," I said. "It's not our job to kill."

"Ridiculous," Scarlet said. "Some people need killing. You can't deny that."

"Maybe so, but today we're just trying to catch a thief. Zoe Willis is the daughter of Gerard Willis."

"The actor?" Rosemarie asked.

"That's the one," I said.

"He's so hot. I wouldn't kick him out of my bed."

"Which one is he?" Scarlet asked.

"Looks great in a tuxedo," I said. "Doesn't shy away from the nude scenes. Little dimple in his chin."

"Oh, yeah," Scarlet said. "I've seen him. He's not bad. They don't make 'em like they did in my day though. Where are the Clark Gables and Errol Flynns? No one knows how to romance anymore. Too much women's lib crap. All the men are too scared to give them flowers because of sexual harassment. I tell you, in my day if a man sent you flowers or romanced you in the moonlight you might as well leave your underpants at home."

"I thought women waited for marriage to have sex in your day," Rosemarie said.

"Pfft," Scarlet said. "That's an old wives' tale. We were just a lot faster picking husbands back then. Try 'em on for size and then make a decision. Bam. All done. Plus, we didn't have birth control so it was kind of a crapshoot. Sometimes you had to take what you could get or convince the other guy it was his baby."

"Yikes," Rosemarie said.

I'd learned to just let Scarlet's stories roll off. "Anyway," I said. "Gerard's daughter has a beach condo on Tybee Island, but she's been cut off from daddy's pocket book. Last month she reported an armed robbery and told police she'd been tied up and assaulted while her condo was ransacked. She had a few abrasions around her wrists and some scratches on her face, but nothing too serious. Between the jewelry and art, almost a million dollars of stuff was taken. She filed a claim with insurance, but insurance isn't buying it that it went down as she said it did. The insurance company hired us to decide whether or not they're going to have to make a million-dollar payout to Miss Willis."

"How are we going to catch her?" Rosemarie said. "A little B&E like that one case you and Kate did? Maybe she's got all the goods hidden away in her safe."

"Nothing that exciting," I said. I was barely proficient at B&E when I was with an expert like Kate. I couldn't imagine what it'd be like with Rosemarie and Scarlet tagging along. "There was an alert from a pawn shop in Charleston where some of the stolen goods were brought in. We're going to check it out and see if the items match up with our list and if the clerk can give a positive ID on whoever brought it in."

"I love going to Charleston," Scarlet said. "I think one of my husbands was from there. Or maybe it was his brother who lived there. Whichever it was, I remember a big white balcony and a bathtub full of vodka."

"Your trips to Charleston and mine are very different," I said.

Chapter Eleven

IT TOOK us a good three hours to get to Charleston, and it was going on four o'clock by the time we arrived.

I found parking on a side street, and I maneuvered Black Betty into the space. Thank goodness there was no one parked behind me, or parallel parking wouldn't have been as easy as I'd made it look.

My phone rang and I didn't recognize the number. "Addison Holmes," I said.

"This is Jolene Meader," the woman said. "You know, from the Good Luck Café?"

"I've know you since I was born, Jolene."

"People forget their roots when they move away," she said. "I don't expect you to be any different."

"What's going on?" I asked.

"I saw that man again," she said. "The one I was telling you about from last fall. Creepy brown eyes."

"When was that?" I asked, grabbing a pen and piece of paper from my bag.

"This morning. Saw him at the drugstore. I've got a girl who opens the café for breakfast now so I don't have to get up so godawful early, but I like to go into the drugstore early. That's when you find out all the juicy bits about people. Who's picking up prescriptions they don't want anyone to know about, buying condoms or pregnancy tests. The early birds usually have something to hide."

"Good to know," I said. "What did creepy brown eyes buy?"

"Lots of packing tape, a couple of bottles of alcohol, scissors, a screwdriver set, a padlock, a home wax kit, and a pack of gum. Cinnamon flavored. There might have been a few more things in his basket, but I couldn't see them."

"Impressive," I said. And a reminder to never buy anything in Whiskey Bayou. "Did you see where he went?"

"He was heading toward Bayou Bridge and driving a beige Cadillac. Older model."

"Was anyone with him?"

"Nope, just him. See you at the party. I always said you and that boy you're marrying are good people."

She hung up, and I shook my head in wonder. I'd never heard Jolene say a good word about anyone.

We all filed out of the van. I was going to say something to Rosemarie and Scarlet about not drawing a lot of attention to ourselves and letting me do the talking, but then I stopped to really look at us and figured it was a waste of breath. We looked like we'd just gotten off the crazy bus—Scarlet in her fur coat and Rosemarie in her puffball hat and too wide anime eyes.

"Let's do this," Scarlet said, and started walking across the street.

I sighed and followed after her.

"I love pawn shops," Rosemarie said. "It's like a store of hidden treasures."

"Or other people's junk," I said.

"When I got divorced I sold my wedding rings to a pawn shop," Rosemarie said. "And all his guns and ammo and most of his clothes. Plus his record collection and his toolbox. He was real mad about that toolbox, but I got a great price on it. I used that money to buy Johnny Castle and Baby. I figured it was the least Roger could do since he got all new stuff when he moved in with that skank."

"What's a skank?" Scarlet asked.

"Like a ho," I said.

"I like the words young people use nowadays. I keep a list of all my favorites. Cray, trolling, catfishing, bae, wizard sleeve... It's like learning a whole new language. I'm bilingual."

"Where did you learn those words?" I asked.

"When I was at the grocery store one day this girl said, "Bitch, you cray," and then I was like, "Damn skippy." And apparently, catfishing is what I was doing when I filled out my online dating profile. I don't photograph as good as I used to, so I used a picture of a young Delta Burke and put a lot of different filters on it to give her that soft dewy look. But I guess that's illegal because they yanked my profile down when that young man complained. He wasn't nothing special anyway. He must've been wearing a toupee in his picture because he was as bald as an egg when he showed up on our date."

"Poor guy," I heard Rosemarie mutter under her breath.

Queen to Pawn was one of the larger pawn shops in the area. It sat just outside downtown Charleston and was located on the corner of a strip of buildings. It took up both floors and had tacky neon signs and arrows pointing to the front door.

I opened the front door and a little bell rang, alerting our arrival. The place was huge and smelled of must and other people's stuff. There were musical instruments against one whole wall, and speakers and amps. There were auto-graphed gold records and vintage movie posters, and big screen TVs on the other side. There was a row of square jewelry counters with glass tops and fronts, and the cheaper pieces were up toward the front of the store and the diamond rings closer to the main counter in the center of the store.

Behind the counter were all the guns—racks and racks of them—and there was a little bald man standing by the register, staring at us like he'd never seen three women coming into a pawn shop before. He was about my height and wearing a long-sleeve plaid shirt with the cuffs rolled up to the elbows. Both his arms and knuckles were tattooed, and his name tag said Daryl.

"I'm gonna look around," Scarlet said. "I've got my eye on that banjo over there."

I looked at Rosemarie, and she shrugged. "I'm sure the people on the cruise ship will love that."

I smiled and then looked at the man behind the counter. "I'm Addison Holmes," I said. "I'm working for Alliance Insurance on a fraud claim, and I saw on the hot sheet that you'd bought some items."

"Actually, the new guy bought the items," he said, his disgust clear to see. "Dummy didn't bother to check the hot sheet first for some primo goods. I noticed it when I was going over the inventory report when I came in just after noon, so I called it in. Cops haven't been here yet. But the new guy is now unemployed. I don't deal in stolen goods in my place. Now I've got to find a new dummy to work for me."

"They like being called dummy?" Rosemarie asked.

The guy shrugged. "Depends on if they deserve it. I mostly say it behind their backs."

"You shouldn't have any problem finding someone new," Rosemarie said, deadpan.

"Do you have the items?" I asked. "I'd like to check them against the list the insurance company gave me."

"Yeah, I put them aside once I realized what they were," Daryl said.

He grabbed a box from under the counter, and then got one of the black velvet rectangles so he could display the jewelry. He took the pieces out one by one and laid them on the velvet.

I opened my file and took out the list and a picture of Zoe Willis. "Do you recognize this girl?" I asked.

He squinted at the picture and shook his head. "I've not seen her before, but I wasn't here when these were brought in. I can check the security camera and have it brought up on the big TVs in the front."

"That would be great, thanks," I said. Rosemarie had wandered off, and I was left there alone to look at each piece of jewelry and see if they matched the descriptions from the insurance company.

"She brought in a couple of pieces of art too," Daryl said. "New guy paid her way too much for that stuff. The dummy. He deserves to be unemployed."

I heard the first strains of "Dueling Banjos" from somewhere behind me, and I grimaced in apology to Daryl.

"I'm going to get the security video set up," he said, and escaped to the back.

From somewhere upstairs came the answering call of "Dueling Banjos", only Rosemarie didn't have a banjo. She was singing in her high operatic soprano.

"Oh, Lord," I whispered and tried to read through the list as fast as possible and check off the matching items.

These were definitely Zoe Willis's belongings. Now I just needed to see if she was dumb enough to bring them in herself. Either way, the insurance company wasn't going to have to shell out the cash, and the ball would be back in their court as to what to do with her about the insurance fraud.

By the time Daryl came back to the counter Scarlet and Rosemarie were in full dueling banjo mode.

"Is that a cat?" he asked, looking toward the stairs that led to the second floor. "I think someone stepped on it."

"Were you able to get the video?" I asked, talking louder to drown out the background noise.

"Yeah, it's pulled up on the TVs in front."

We walked to the front of the store where the big screen TVs were and the screens were all blue. I could see Scarlet from where we stood in front of the TVs and she'd tossed her mink over a sousaphone. Daryl seemed a little shell-shocked. I was guessing he'd never seen a ninety-something year old woman with hair extensions rocking out on a banjo. I hadn't even known she could play.

She looked up at us while Rosemarie was singing her part of the song and gave us the devil horns sign and stuck out her tongue like Gene Simmons.

"This won't take long," I told Daryl.

He snapped out of his trance and turned toward the TVs. He had a remote in his hand and he pointed it toward a little black box I hadn't noticed before attached to the ceiling. When he hit play the screens lit up with the security tape, and he fast-forwarded until Zoe Willis came into the store.

"That's her," I said. "Can I have a copy to give to the insurance company?"

"Sure, no problem."

"I'm going to take this banjo too," Scarlet said. "But I'm not paying five hundred dollars. What'll you take for it?"

Daryl didn't miss a beat. "Whatever you think it's worth. It's yours. Please take it."

"See, Addison. The art of the deal. I'm an expert."

I nodded and waited while Scarlet dug a hundred dollars out of the pocket of her mink and left it on the counter. I finally understood how she'd been a successful spy. She'd just worn people down until they'd either killed themselves or turned themselves in. It all made sense now.

Rosemarie came back downstairs with several porcelain dolls, and I remembered she collected them. They were all over her duplex, and I'd once mistakenly gone into her guest bedroom instead of the bathroom and screamed because of all the creepy doll eyes staring at me. Between the dogs and the dolls, Rosemarie didn't have a lot of house guests.

Daryl came back and handed me a disc of the security footage, and he rang up Rosemarie's dolls. Scarlet had wandered off again, picking at her banjo and browsing the aisles. The bell dinged above the door and someone walked in with two boxes, one stacked on top of the other.

I couldn't see a face because the boxes covered it up, but when she shifted to the side to put her boxes on one of the counters I realized it was Zoe Willis, back for a second run. Lord, she was a dummy. She must've had no idea how the system worked for pawning stolen goods. And the fact she'd gotten away with it the first time because the clerk was a dummy too just made her more bold.

I took a step back and got my phone out so I could take a couple of pictures, just to seal the deal. I could tell Daryl recognized her, but he was playing it cool, continuing to ring up Rosemarie's dolls.

The problem with having a choir teacher and a geriatric spy as sidekicks is that one of them doesn't understand the element of surprise and the other one understands it but has reached the age she doesn't care.

Rosemarie gasped, her Cupid's bow mouth making a perfect oval, and she stared straight at Zoe Willis. Zoe took a step back and turned her head so she looked directly at me, where my camera was still up and clearly taking pictures of her. This was enough to spook her, and she started running for the front door.

It didn't matter. We weren't cops. We weren't there to arrest her. We got all the proof we needed, and the insurance company and local police could sort out the rest. It should have been that simple. But Scarlet jumped out in front of her, wielding her banjo like a sword.

"You're going down, sucker," she yelled, swinging the banjo again.

Zoe hopped back out of the way and I went forward to try and contain Scarlet before she hurt herself or someone else. But Zoe must've thought I was coming for her because she turned and sucker-punched me right in the face.

"Ouch," I yelled, covering my face with my hands. "Son of a b—"

My nose was gushing blood and my vision blurred, but I heard Scarlet let out a war cry and the smash of the banjo as she took out Zoe at the knees and the girl went crashing down.

Rosemarie brought me a handful of tissues to stifle the bleeding and said, "Your face is really going to clash with your dress come Friday."

Chapter Twelve

WEDNESDAY

My alarm went off at six the next morning, and at first I thought someone had put a cinder block on my face sometime during the night. My face hurt. Bad. And I couldn't quite open my eyes. That probably wasn't a good sign.

Nick hadn't made it home the night before, which was probably a good thing. This seemed like the type of news that was delivered best through text message. I'd slept with an ice pack on my face in hopes the swelling would go down. I wasn't sure it had done much good, but at least I could breathe.

I got out of bed and shuffled off to the bathroom, feeling old for the first time in my life. I didn't like getting punched in the face. I didn't like getting punched anywhere. Or falling or getting knocked down on purpose. It hurt. And I could definitely feel the changes in my body as I got older. I didn't bounce back as quickly as I used to.

I walked right past the mirror and to the shower to turn it on, not quite ready to face the facts about looking like Quasimodo in my wedding pictures. I groaned and put my face against the cold tile on the wall. I didn't even have a wedding photographer *to* take pictures. A couple of tears escaped and I sniffed. I was tougher than this. Stronger than this. I could overcome any obstacle. Except it felt like everything was working against us.

I stripped out of my nightshirt and stood there naked while steam filled the bathroom. I hoped it would lessen the blow when I turned to look in the mirror. It didn't. I gasped at the sight of my face and immediately burst into tears. My nose was swollen and I had two black eyes.

Crying didn't help anything because I couldn't breathe again, so I got into the shower and tried to come up with an alternative plan. I went through every scenario in my head, from wearing a mask to getting an emergency facelift. And then I thought about calling off the wedding altogether and bit my lip. I should've eloped.

I finished showering and dried off quickly, not bothering to spend any more time dwelling on something I couldn't change. Mostly I couldn't stand to look in the mirror again because I was afraid the tears would keep coming.

I dressed in black leggings and a soft black sweater because the day seemed to call for mourning, and I grabbed my things to head to the office early. I was just reaching Telfair Square and looking for my usual parking spot when Savage called.

"Got your message," he said. "We need to talk."

"I'm just pulling up to the agency."

"Me too," he said and then hung up.

I raised my brows in surprise, but it hurt too much so I relaxed my face again. Whatever information Savage had must have been good.

He pulled up behind me in his black Tahoe, and he was waiting on the sidewalk before I could get out of the van.

"What does the other guy look like?" he said, examining my face.

"I don't know. She's in jail for the time being. But she doesn't look as bad as me. Scarlet only managed to kneecap her with a banjo."

Savage's lips quirked. "She's losing her touch. She usually goes for the head."

"The girl was kind of tall. It's no longer my problem, thank God. The cops and the insurance company can figure it out. I didn't press charges. She's going to have enough to deal with. And, of course, Scarlet hightailed it out of there before the cops came because she's a person of interest in Big Mo's murder. I haven't seen her since."

He stayed silent and just stared at me, looking pained.

"What?" I asked.

"I don't know what to say. Everything that pops into my head seems like a bad idea."

"Probably a good idea to say nothing. I'm trying not to

think about what my face is going to look like in wedding pictures."

"Maybe just keep the veil down the whole time."

I hadn't thought of that.

"What did Nick say?" he asked, following me up the agency stairs to the front doors. It was still early, and the doors were locked, so I used my key to get in.

"He doesn't know yet. I figured I'd text him later and then give him a few hours to get used to the idea before he sees me in person."

I saw his mouth quirk again, and I headed straight into the conference room to get coffee started. There were some trays of fruit in the fridge, but I passed it over for the left-over brownies someone hadn't finished from the day before's pastry box.

"Brownies for breakfast?" he asked, wincing as I heated them in the microwave.

"Don't judge. I deserve these brownies. What's up with the cryptic phone call?" I asked.

"I was going to wait until you had your coffee. I know how you get."

I narrowed my eyes at him, but realized he'd spent enough time around me to know me well. I always forgot he had psychology training and observed people on a level they probably weren't always comfortable with.

The conference room was more spacious than my office, so I took a seat in one of the plush chairs and propped my boots on the table while I let the coffee infiltrate my bloodstream.

"The secretary at the church in Whiskey Bayou emailed me all the personnel files of employees over the last ten years. I wasn't really sure where to start as far as this stalker goes and figured it might be someone he worked with, either past or present."

"Makes sense," Savage said, grabbing a bottle of water from the mini fridge and then taking a seat across from me.

I filled him in on my first conversation with the man who'd answered the phone and how he'd said that Tilda Sweeney no longer worked for the church, and then I filled him in on my conversation with Tilda Sweeney.

"I brought the coroner's report," he said, pushing over a file. Whatever was in it was a heck of a lot more than a coroner's report. It was at least two inches thick.

"What's all this?" I asked.

"A huge mess," he said. "And a lot of people a lot higher up than me asking a lot of questions."

"I don't like dealing with people higher up than you," I said.

"Believe me, I'm not too fond of it either. Fifteen years ago, a man named Carlos Rodriguez orchestrated a huge drug deal down in Miami. The drugs belonged to Frank Cardonas, and Rodriguez got busted with more than thirty-million dollars' worth of cocaine. He wouldn't turn on Cardonas. That's who we really wanted. But Rodriguez was scared shitless of him and he should have been. Cardonas had his own wife tortured and killed, and then he impaled her body on a pike in the closest town to his compound. Everyone was scared of him."

"Geez," I said, the brownie not settling all that well in my stomach.

"Rodriguez was pretty much a dead man walking. Everybody knew it. Cardonas never let any of his men that were captured live long, even if they didn't squeal. Rodriguez was pretty high up in the organization, so he had inside information about Cardonas that we didn't. So Rodriguez was offered a deal in witness protection if he'd turn on Cardonas. And he took the deal."

"Are you saying that Carlos Rodriguez and Pastor Charles are the same person?" I asked.

"That's what I'm saying. Rodriguez went into the program under the name Charles Gaspar, and after he'd testified and members of the cartel started going down, he was relocated to Omaha, Nebraska. He was given his start-up money while he looked for a job, but he never found anything that stuck. Odd jobs here and there. He checked in with his Marshal like clockwork, never missed a phone call or a visit, until one day he did. By then there was no sign of him anywhere."

"What about the real Pastor Charles?" I asked.

"It turned out Rodriguez had been doing some day labor work at the church. That's as close a proximity as we can put him with Charles Whidbey. I'm guessing at that point Rodriguez started planning his escape. He waited until Whidbey took his sabbatical so he'd have plenty of time to set things up without too many people wondering where the pastor went. He sent a very nice letter of resignation to the church board, explaining that he felt God was calling him elsewhere and that he had to go. And then he took on Whidbey's identity and buried his body out in a ravine. He kept Whidbey's personal belongings—photographs of his wife—anything that would convince people that he was in fact Charles Whidbey."

"So whose number was it on the reference sheet that I called today?"

"Don't know," Savage said. "But I'm guessing he had someone from the cartel he kept in touch with. Someone he trusted. If you'll give me the numbers we can trace them and try to track them down."

"Couldn't be someone too trustworthy," I said. "After all that trouble and deception someone still found him."

"That's the thing about cartels. Anyone and anything can be bought for a price. The Cardonas cartel ran far and wide. Even with the testimony Rodriguez gave, there are still arrests being made to this day. But my guess is it's Cardonas's brother who's coming after Rodriguez. There was never any lost love between them, and now that Frank Cardonas is behind bars, the cartel falls to his brother, Emile. He's just not as good at it, and it's unravelling at the seams. He's doing such a bad job that we don't even have to put all our resources into hunting them down anymore. Emile is doing the work for us unintentionally."

"You have a picture of him?" I asked.

"Probably. I'll see what I can dig up."

"I think he's in Whiskey Bayou. I got a call from Jolene Meader yesterday, and she said she saw a man she remembers coming in the café last fall. He stood out because he had creepy eyes, and he's back in town. The pictures Pastor Charles gave me were taken over the last several months. Emile could've been under his nose this whole time without too many people noticing."

"If Emile's been toying with him this long he's probably getting ready to finish Rodriguez off. Especially if he knows he came to see you. More than likely, there are probably bugs in his home and office at the church. Emile likes to play, like a cat with a mouse."

I was having trouble processing the fact that a man who'd been a beloved pastor in our small town for the past ten years was a drug runner and murderer. And then I had another thought.

"Ohmigod," I said, the bottom dropping from my stomach. "He's not a real pastor. He can't marry us."

"Not to mention the fact he's a criminal and will go to jail for murder if he's not already dead."

I couldn't control the tears this time. I was a mess. I was never this emotional. "The wedding is doomed." And then I dropped my head onto the table and sobbed.

"As long as you've got your marriage license anyone who's ordained can marry you," Savage said. "I'm sure we can find someone."

I lifted my head up and he winced at the sight of me. I must have looked bad because he didn't even have a joke.

"I forgot about the marriage license," I said. "We don't have one." And then I started sobbing again.

"I can't help you there," he said. "And I don't mean this to come out the wrong way, but you seem more nuts than usual."

"It's the wedding hormones," I said.

"It's some kind of hormones, but I don't know if it's wedding related. You need to take a chill pill. Or eat some ice cream. Otherwise you'll end up sitting on the edge of the Talmadge Bridge and someone will have to climb up and talk you down. It's a safety risk to everyone."

The crying hadn't helped. It just made my face hurt worse and I couldn't breathe again. "Ice cream," I said.

"There you go."

Savage got up and then leaned down and kissed me on the top of the head, and then he disappeared.

Chapter Thirteen

AN HOUR LATER, I was feeling a little better. I'd washed my face and laid on my office floor with an ice bag until I could breathe again. I decided the pity party was over. Savage was right. If I didn't get myself under control I'd end up on the ledge of the bridge, and nobody looked good after jumping off that thing.

I decided to call Nick and let him know what was going on. It's not like I could hide it from him until after we were married, though the thought had crossed my mind. I also needed him so we could go to the courthouse and get our marriage license.

"Hey, Siri," I said to my phone. I waited for the little beep and then said, "Call Nick."

"Calling Rick."

"Rick? Who's Rick? No, call Nick."

"Calling Vicki."

I sighed. "Stupid thing. Can't you understand English?"

My phone rang before I could call Nick the old-fashioned way, and I saw it was my mother.

"We're back," she said as a greeting. "I think someone broke into the house while we were gone. All the junk food is gone and there are rolling papers next to the bathtub."

I pressed my lips together. "Did you have a good trip?"

"It was nice to get away. It's the only recourse I have when Scarlet comes to town. I spent thirty years having to put up with her when your father was alive, but now that he's gone I can get the hell out of Dodge. It's either that or kill her."

"I'm glad you had a good time," I said.

"Have you seen your sister?"

"Nope, last I heard she had to go paint."

"Is the wedding still on?"

I was silent for a few seconds. Someone must have already told her about my face. It was impossible to keep secrets from my mother. "Is there any reason it wouldn't be?"

"Just curious," she said, her voice unusually high. "Is there anything you need me to do? I hope you don't mind that I'm recycling the dress I wore at your last wedding. I didn't figure I should go to the expense of getting another one when that one has hardly been worn."

"Good thinking," I said.

"You could've done that with your wedding dress, and

saved yourself a fortune. I've heard how much those dresses at Le Couture are."

"Nothing to worry about. Nina and Aunt Scarlet picked up the tab."

My mother was silent as she contemplated what that meant. "Is it anything I want to know about?"

"Nope, water under the bridge."

I said goodbye to my mom and then called Nick.

"You must have left early this morning," he said. "I just got home and you were gone."

I dodged a bullet there. I could imagine how pissed he'd be if he'd come home and found me looking like Michael Jackson from the "Thriller" video.

"We should probably talk about a couple of things," I said.

"Should I sit down for this?" he asked.

"Not necessary. But maybe don't get too comfortable. We haven't gotten our marriage license. I totally forgot we needed one."

Nick blew out a breath. "I forgot too. I can meet you at the courthouse in half an hour. I should probably shower first."

"And maybe we could get our wedding bands while we're out. And ice cream."

"What are you not telling me?" he asked.

"My face might look a tiny bit different when you see me. But don't be alarmed. I can wear my veil. Or a mask."

"How different?"

"Remember when we saw Mickey Rourke that day in Charleston, and we weren't sure if it was him or not?"

"Damn," he said. "What happened?"

"It wasn't my fault," I assured him.

"It usually isn't. You're just a magnet for disaster."

"I was trying to keep Aunt Scarlet from assaulting this girl who's going to jail for insurance fraud, but the girl thought I was coming after her instead of Scarlet, so she punched me in the face. The good news is my nose isn't broken."

He sighed again. I was a trial. "I'll see you at the courthouse."

When I hung up the phone I was feeling a little better. Nick had a calming effect on me, probably because nothing ever really got him bent out of shape. He let things roll off his back. Unless they didn't, and then it was best to get out of the way.

I grabbed my emergency makeup kit from my bag and put my concealer to good use. It didn't make a huge difference, but my nose didn't look so red and swollen. I put on a little extra eyeliner and mascara and smudged it some, so maybe people would think I was just going for an extreme smoky eye look.

By the time I was finished, it was almost time to meet Nick. I put my coat on and a pair of sunglasses, and headed to Kate's office to let her know I'd be out. When I got to the end of the hall I saw her door was closed and the light was off. I'd forgotten she was stuck in court all week testifying. Better her than me.

The courthouse was literally across the street from the agency, so I turned my completed files over to a silent Lucy on the way out and cut through Telfair Square. Nick was already waiting for me on the front steps.

He was wearing dark-gray slacks and a light-blue, button-down shirt. His badge was clipped at his waist, and he wore a black wool overcoat. His lips pressed together tighter the closer I got, and when I stood right in front of him he carefully removed my sunglasses.

"Weirdly enough, this isn't the worst I've seen you," he said.

"And you're marrying me anyway," I said, leaning in to kiss him gently. "Maybe everyone inside will think you're forcing me to marry you. Should I slip someone a note that says *Help, I'm being kidnapped*?"

"Not funny," he said. "I'm already going to take flak from the guys once they hear about this. Your story better be credible for how this happened."

"Easy enough. Scarlet hit a woman with a banjo, and then the woman punched me."

"Yeah, that's totally credible. Let's get this done."

He took my elbow and led me up the stairs and inside. We went through the security process and they locked up Nick's weapon so we could go through the metal detectors. Every person we passed stared at me and then scowled at Nick. I put my sunglasses back on.

It turns out getting a marriage license isn't that complicated. What dragged it out was the poor woman behind the counter who kept sending Nick on errands and then asking me over and over again if I needed help, or if she could give me the number for a woman's shelter. I appreciated the Good Samaritan in her, but I was really needing that ice cream and she was holding me back.

By the time we left, Nick's jaw was clamped tight and the little vein in his temple was throbbing.

"We can take my unit to finish up," he said. "Black Betty doesn't exactly scream low profile. We're already getting enough stares."

"No one who knows you would ever think you did something like this to me," I said, trying to reassure him. "This isn't the first time I've had a black eye. I'm sure it won't be the last."

"That's very comforting," he said.

Nick was driving his truck today, and it was big and black and the headlights bulged like bug eyes. While I was gracefully hitching myself into the passenger seat, I had a thought about Pastor Charles and the information that Savage had given me. I wasn't using my greatest strengths to my advantage in solving this case. Despite the fact that Pastor Charles was a murderer and wasn't actually a real preacher, he still belonged to Whiskey Bayou. At least until everyone found out the truth.

I scrolled through my phone until I found the number Jolene Meader had called me from. She answered on the first ring.

"Jolene, this is Addison Holmes."

"Yeah?"

"This case I'm working on is a real head-scratcher. You see, Pastor Charles is having a little trouble with a stalker."

Jolene gasped and said, "Get out of town. You think it's that guy?"

"I think it very well could be. The guy keeps leaving Pastor Charles photographs of himself. He even broke into his house and left some on the nightstand."

"I told you he had creepy eyes. Creepiest eyes I've ever seen. Dead inside if you ask me. Who would do such a thing to a preacher of all people?"

"That's what Pastor Charles hired me to find out. But in the meantime, we can't let this man get away with what he's doing."

"Nobody messes with our preachers. I'll kick his ass the next time I see him."

"Maybe don't do that," I said, wishing I'd thought a little farther ahead in my plan. "He's armed and dangerous."

"Don't matter none to me," she said. "I got that sawed-off under the counter. I'll put a hole right through his face and go back to serving pie."

"Hmm," I said. "Do you think you can put the word out about this man? What he's driving? I'll text you a picture of him and you can pass it around. Everyone needs to look out for Pastor Charles, but without letting Pastor Charles know we're looking out for him."

"Got it," she said. "He sure does have a lot of pride for a preacher. He should probably repent about that."

"I'll pass it on to him next time I hear from him."

Jolene disconnected, and Nick was staring at me. "I feel like I've missed something important," he said.

"We've run into a slight hiccup with the wedding," I said. "We don't actually have anyone to marry us. It turns out Pastor Charles isn't really a pastor after all. His name is Carlos Rodriguez and he killed the real Pastor Charles and took over his identity."

"That seems like more than a slight hiccup."

"I'm sure we can find someone to marry us. Everyone is ordained nowadays. I was watching *Pitbulls and Parolees* on Animal Planet the other day, and one of the dogs was ordained."

"Why hasn't Pastor Charles been arrested?"

"We can't find him," I said. "He's a slippery devil. Savage is all over this case. Turns out the fake Pastor Charles used to be in WITSEC and flipped on Frank Cardonas."

Nick whistled long and low. "I'm guessing Frank is a little pissed since he'll be behind bars the rest of his life."

"You could say that," I said. "The physical description Jolene gave me of a guy she's seen around town fits the description of Frank's brother. At this point, we need to find Pastor Charles before Emile does."

"What makes you think Pastor Charles hasn't gone into hiding?" Nick asked.

"He's been checking in with his secretary. His car is parked outside the rectory. Maybe he's hoping I would do enough to stop whoever has found him without digging too deep. I'd think you'd reach a point in your life where you'd want to stop running and constantly looking over your shoulder all the time."

"He's underestimated you," Nick said. "And he's using you to get rid of his problem, and assuming you're not good enough to dig too deep into his past."

"I wouldn't have been able to dig back so far without Savage."

"It's good to have friends in the right places," he said.

He parked the truck in front of the jewelry store, and I sighed. "I don't suppose you know a preacher who can perform a last-minute ceremony."

"It depends on if you want the marriage to be legal."

"I'll let you know."

The jewelry store was right next to the ice cream shop, and I looked back and forth between them, not sure which I wanted first.

"The ice cream shop doesn't open for another half hour. Rings first. Then ice cream."

"I love it when you're decisive." I walked my fingers up his sleeve, feeling very warm in some very interesting places. I moved in close and he arched a brow, his full attention on me. "I could be persuaded to skip ice cream for a different kind of dessert."

Nick reached up and took my sunglasses from the top of my head and put them on my eyes. "And I could be persuaded into eating two desserts. Maybe. The black eyes are throwing me off my game."

"We should've brought Black Betty," I said, grabbing his hand and dragging him toward the jewelry store. "That's a multipurpose van."

Nick and I were no strangers to DeLuce's. We'd worked a case last year that had involved stolen Russian diamonds and a dead courier, and Christian DeLuce had been right in the thick of things. Fortunately, he'd been cleared so he was free to continue to make the beautiful jewelry designs he was famous for. We'd gotten my engagement ring from Christian, though it hadn't been for the purpose of being engaged at the time.

We walked through the door, and Nick nodded at the security guard who sat on a stool to the left. There was one other couple in the store, and they were bent over looking into one of the cases.

"Detective Dempsey," Christian DeLuce called out as soon as he saw us.

He was a bird-like, flamboyant man with thinning strawberry-blond hair and the palest skin I'd ever seen. He was close to fifty in age, but looked much younger, and his eyes were the palest of blues.

"Oh, my," he said, rushing up to kiss both of my cheeks, but he stopped at the sight of my face. "Good Lord, what happened to you?" I removed the sunglasses and he gasped audibly. And then he looked at Nick.

"I had a small incident while on a case," I said.

He cut his eyes back toward Nick like he was expecting him to start throwing punches. "Well, in any case, it's so lovely to see both of you again. I hope you're here for pleasure and not because of dead bodies. I've bought no foreign gems lately."

The people at the counter turned and looked at us, and I smiled and said, "He's kidding."

"We're here for wedding bands," Nick said.

Something in my brain clicked and I realized I recognized the woman at the counter. Her name was Heather Labo, and her husband had hired us to see if she was having an affair. The man she was with was definitely not her husband. And as if on cue, she reached down and patted his butt.

"A wedding," Christian said, clapping his hands. "How exciting. I, of course, have the loveliest bands. When is the big day? A summer wedding, perhaps? Fall?"

"It's Friday," I said, following him to the counter on the opposite side of the store. DeLuce's only dealt in high-end jewelry, and they were known for their rare and exclusive pieces. DeLuce was the jeweler to the stars and most of the world's billionaires.

"I'm sorry, what?" he asked, somehow managing to look even more pale.

"Yes," I said. "It's all been put together very fast. I've only had a week to plan."

Christian looked down at my waistline and raised his brows.

"And not because of that," I said, offended. "We just don't want to wait."

"Hmm," he said, clearly not believing me. "You'll wear your veil, I suppose."

I narrowed my eyes at him, but it hurt too much so it wasn't very effective.

"I just don't know what I can do," he said, waving his hands. "I keep a selection, of course, but not in all sizes. Most of our bands are custom-made and unique in some way."

He was getting all flustered and clearly upset at the thought of selling us something plain.

"Just show us whatever you have," Nick told him and Christian walked off to the back room, shaking his head and muttering about people expecting him to work miracles.

I took the opportunity to put my bag on the counter and dig through it until I found the file on Heather Labo.

"What are you doing?" Nick asked.

I opened the file and showed him the picture paper-clipped to the front.

He sighed. "Of course this would happen. I forgot who I was with."

"If you help me do this now I'll do that thing you like during second dessert."

He arched a brow at that. "Which thing? The thing you sometimes do, or the thing you almost never do?"

"The thing I almost never do," I said.

"I'm in. But you realize I'm supposed to be working on a case right now."

"What would you be doing if you were working right now?" I asked, curiously.

"Banging my head against a wall trying to get warrants."

"My thing seems like more fun," I said.

"Yeah, you're right. The case is out of my hands right now. My grandfather is pulling some strings. I just need to be patient and let him work his magic. He'll get to the bottom of things. Money always talks." Nick subtly looked at the couple at the other counter. "I take it that isn't her husband?"

"Right on the first try. She's married to Martin Labo, and there's about a thirty-year age difference and no prenup on the line."

"Yikes," Nick said. "Bet he's regretting that one."

"He seems to have many regrets. Like marrying her at all."

"She reminds me of someone," Nick said.

"She's like a generic *Real Housewives of Orange County*. Big lips, big boobs, too much tan, and fabulous shoes. Looks like she's getting a new bauble."

"Do you know who the man is?" Nick asked.

"No, never seen him before."

"He works in the DA's office. Up-and-coming attorney with political aspirations. I've seen him in passing, but we don't know each other on a personal level."

"He's wearing a wedding ring, too," I said. "Sometimes I hate this job."

Nick squeezed my hand and I put the file away when Christian came back with a tray of only four rings. I was having trouble focusing on them because I kept sneaking glances at Heather. A woman like that would never be satisfied with what she had. There would always be something just out of her grasp and she'd throw everything away with the hopes of getting just a little more. In the end she'd be left with no one—alone and withered—until people forgot she ever existed. It was sad, really.

"Ms. Holmes?" Christian said, clearly having tried to get my attention multiple times.

"I'm sorry, I've got a lot on my mind."

"Of course you do," he said. "I couldn't imagine throwing a wedding together in a week. I couldn't throw a dinner party together in a week. How many people will be attending?"

I thought about the small wedding for friends and family that had somehow turned into a block party for an entire town and said, "Around three thousand. It's open bar."

Which reminded me that I needed to ask Rosemarie if she'd been able to secure plenty of booze. The last thing we wanted was a bunch of angry, almost drunk townspeople. They'd burn Whiskey Bayou to the ground.

Christian choked and went into a dramatic fit of coughing. "Well," he finally said. "You're both much braver than I could ever be, that's for sure. Now take a look at these rings. I just happen to have two matching sets in your sizes."

"That one," Nick and I both said at the same time, pointing to the plain silver bands.

"I guess that's a match," Christian said. "Oh, I do love weddings. So romantic. I consider myself in the wedding business. So many repeat customers. You really get to know people on a personal level."

"I bet," I said. "We'd love to have you at ours if you're free."

"Oh, I wish I could," he said sympathetically. "It sounds like it could be a real spectacle. But I've got to fly off to Italy for a show. You can pick the rings up on Friday morning before the wedding. My assistant will be here." He pointed to the woman who was helping Heather Labo select a necklace and matching earrings.

I didn't have an excuse for sticking around and waiting for Heather and her lover to finish up, so Nick and I left and he turned toward the ice cream shop.

"I'll wait in the car if you'll get mine," I said. "I don't want to miss them if they leave. I'll only have one more case to wrap up before the end of the week if I can get this done."

He reluctantly handed me the truck keys and said, "What do you want?"

"Triple hot fudge sundae. Extra sauce and whipped cream."

"How you don't weigh four hundred pounds I'll never know."

"Good metabolism. By the time I'm Scarlet's age think of how small I'll be. I'll have practically shrunk to nothing."

"If I ever get to be Scarlet's age I'd prefer you just take me in the backyard and shoot me."

"We should probably make some adjustments in our estate planning."

We knuckle-bumped and I headed toward the truck. I turned on the heater and then got my long-range Nikon out of my bag. Sometimes a camera phone wouldn't do it.

I was able to zoom in and get a couple of clear shots of them at the jewelry counter, but Heather and her lover never turned their faces completely toward the camera. They finally wrapped up their purchase and came out just before Nick did with our ice cream.

"Hurry," I said once he got in the car and handed over my sundae. I looked at his single dip of chocolate and shook my head. I was glad he had more imagination in the bedroom than he did in ice cream choices.

"They're getting into that Mercedes down there. The one that looks like it belongs to a Stormtrooper. I didn't realize working in the DA's office paid so well. That's an expensive car."

"They don't pay that well," Nick said. "Maybe he's got family money."

"I guess he'd have to if he's got political aspirations. And that was no cheap piece of jewelry he just bought for her either. We've got to follow them," I said.

"Addison…"

"Come on, you're going to lose them." I got my laptop out and connected it to my hotspot, and then I ran the license plate on the Mercedes. "It's registered to a Julia Petrie."

"Petrie," Nick said, nodding his head. "That's his name. I couldn't remember. Not sure of his first name. I want to say John or James. Something with a J."

"Jerrod," I said. "Looks like the money comes from his wife's side. I'm sure she'll appreciate knowing what it's going toward."

"They're heading out of the city," Nick said, turning left onto Bay Street and then merging onto the highway and heading toward Chatham.

"You're really good at tailing someone," I said, appreciating how he was able to keep cars between them and us and not lose them in the process.

He spared me a glance. "Thanks," he said dryly.

I was down to the bottom of my sundae and was all but ready to lick the bottom of the plastic container, but decided the stakes were too high at the moment. I put down the container and grabbed my Nikon, and then I zoomed in through the back window of the SUV.

"Where'd she go?" I asked, only seeing the back of Jerrod's head behind the wheel.

"Where do you think she went?" Nick asked. "If you hadn't been so preoccupied with your ice cream you would've noticed she hasn't sat upright the entire car ride."

Jerrod was swerving between the lanes and he finally cut across three lanes of traffic, causing cars to slam on their brakes and honk their horns. He was driving like an idiot.

"Oh," I said, finally realizing why. "I guess that's his reward for the jewelry. They'd better pace themselves. He's going to have a wreck."

"They're getting off here," Nick said. "No pun intended."

I snorted out a laugh as he maneuvered his way across traffic to take the exit ramp.

"Looks like a bunch of middle income neighborhoods," I said.

Nick slowed down and waited until they'd turned onto Magnolia Street before following.

"Look," I said, pointing. "They're turning into that driveway." The garage door opened and the Mercedes disappeared inside.

I typed in the address on the computer. "Looks like a rent house. It's owned by Arthur Coolidge, LLC. I can't tell who's currently renting it."

Nick blew out a breath. "Arthur Coolidge is the DA. They probably all use it for whatever trysts or illegal activities are happening in that office. They're all dirty as hell."

"That's terrible," I said.

"It is what it is. Corruption at its finest. All we can do is our job and collect pieces of information. Maybe one day we'll have enough information for a lot of people to go down. Right now, we don't have it."

"I'm starting to think we should move for real. This place has issues."

"All places have issues. No one is honest anymore. Everyone is in it for themselves and whatever serves their best interest. It's one of the reasons my grandfather wants to retire. He doesn't feel like he can make a difference anymore."

"Maybe you should run for his seat," I said, and then wondered what the hell I was thinking.

But Nick didn't say anything. He just made a U-turn at the end of the street and then parked a few houses down from where Heather and Jerrod went. Almost all the driveways were empty since it was still the middle of the workday.

"Do what you've got to do," he said. "I can't go with you."

"It's a shame because you could boost me over that fence. Good thing there are trees in the backyard."

Nick closed his eyes and shook his head. "I could get fired for this."

"You're right," I said. "You stay here. I'll be right back. Lickety-split."

"I'm not letting you climb fences and trees by yourself. I'd prefer to get married to a live person on Friday."

"I can do this. Really," I said. "I don't want you to get in trouble. And you're dressed kind of fancy."

He just gave me a look that said I'd do best not to argue with him, and I figured he must *really* want me to do that thing I almost never did. "Get your camera."

I strapped it around my neck and hopped out of the car. I watched as Nick took off his long wool coat and put it in the back cab, instead grabbing his black Northface jacket. He grabbed my hand and pulled me along toward the rent house, just a couple out for a stroll in freezing temperatures.

"We'll get in through this one," he said. "Take a couple of pictures and then we'll go around back."

It was then I realized what he was doing. The house next door had a For Sale sign in the front yard. I took a couple of random shots of a traditional two-story brick house with nice big trees in the front and back. There was a realtor's lockbox on the front door, and there were no blinds or curtains in the front windows so people could look into the house. It was staged perfectly, so I was guessing no one currently lived there.

I moseyed casually behind Nick as we walked around the side of the house, and he opened the gate to the backyard like he had every right to be there. Once we were through he closed the gate and did a quick look around. There was a big tree close to the fence that looked like it would be simple enough to climb and then drop down into the yard next door.

"Oh, man," I said. "I hate trees."

"I'll go first," Nick said. And he climbed up the tree like a monkey, took a good look at the yard next door to make sure there was nothing there, and then hopped down and out of sight.

I sighed and hung my camera around my neck, and then I started the climb up the tree. The problem with my gorgeous and practical winter boots was they weren't all that practical for tree climbing. I hauled myself up to the limb that Nick had crossed on, completely out of breath and reminding myself to start exercising again. I'd pretty much stopped after I'd passed the physical fitness portion of my P.I. exam. Apparently you're supposed to keep it up.

"Come on," Nick hissed. He held out a hand for me, but it looked like an awfully long way down.

I crawled out farther onto the limb and it started to bend some, and then a little more. I was wrapped around it like a possum, and I swung upside down, holding on for dear life.

"What now?" I hissed back.

"Just let go. I'll catch you."

"Are you nuts? I'm upside down. I'll break my head."

"Just do it," he said. "They're probably already finished by now."

That thought kicked me into gear and I let go suddenly, reaching for Nick as I came down. He caught me with an *oomph* and staggered back a few steps and then set me on my feet.

"Thanks," I said.

"Let's not do that again."

"Usually when I'm stuck in a tree I'm with Savage or Kate."

"Does that make it better?"

I thought back to those times and shook my head. "Not really," I said. "Pretty much the same outcome."

I got myself together as best I could and then made my way toward the house, staying away from the windows. The backyard was a good size and there was a nice outdoor patio and deck, along with a hot tub.

"Gross, I can only imagine what that poor hot tub has seen."

"You don't know the half of it," Nick said. "You haven't seen the guys at the DA's office. There's not enough bleach in the world to clean that thing."

I shuddered in disgust and looked in the first window I came across. I could barely see through the slats in the blinds, but I could make out what looked to be a small guest bedroom. Nick had been right, they'd been using this place as some kind of DA frat house. The bed took up almost the whole room and all I could see was a lot of black satin and a weird chandelier.

The back of the house was pretty open and I could see into the living room and kitchen area. But there was no sign of Heather and Jerrod.

"You think they even made it out of the garage?" I asked.

"Maybe not," he said. And then he moved in closer to the window so his face was almost pressed against it.

My heart was beating a hundred miles a minute.

"Look there," he said.

I came up next to him and followed where his fingers were pointing. A trail of clothes led through the living room and kitchen into what I was guessing was the master bedroom.

"Come on," I said, and made my way toward the three bay windows. The blinds were closed and I couldn't see inside, not even a speck of light. But there were three narrow, rectangular windows above each of the bay windows. "You're going to have to boost me up."

Nick closed his eyes again and looked to be counting to ten. Then he started over. I smacked him on the shoulder and gestured toward the windows. He rolled his eyes and then knelt so I could sit on his shoulders, and then he slowly came to a standing position. My feet were tucked behind his back and I wobbled back and forth on his shoulders.

"Let go of my hair," he hissed, and I realized I had a death grip on his hair.

"Sorry," I said and tried to sit up straighter. I was right at eye-level with the window, and it surprised me when I actually saw Jerrod and Heather in the room. And boy did I see them. I brought the camera up and took a couple of quick shots. And then I tapped Nick on the top of the head and leaned down.

"Hey, I don't think you have to worry about this guy having

too many political aspirations. He's dressed in a red lace bra and panty set. It's just like the one I have that you like."

"You should probably burn that," Nick said. "Are you done?"

"Almost." I popped back up to get another couple of shots, and Jerrod must have caught movement from the corner of his eye because he turned and we made eye contact.

"Oh, shit," I said, and kicked my foot in Nick's kidney like I was spurring on a horse. "He saw me. Go! Go!"

The last thing I'd seen through the window was both of them scrambling for clothes. They were coming for us.

"Get down and run," Nick said.

But I was frozen, and I had a death grip on Nick's head and my legs were wrapped around him like an anaconda. I wasn't going anywhere. So he started running. I bounced on his shoulders as he plowed through the gate and across the front yard.

"Move your hand," he yelled. "You're covering my eyes."

I was laughing hysterically. I couldn't seem to stop and couldn't seem to get control of myself. I imagined we looked like an ostrich weaving back and forth, running willy-nilly down the street.

Nick opened the driver's side door and tossed me inside, and then shoved me across to the passenger seat. I was completely useless because I couldn't stop laughing and Nick somehow managed to get the car started and speed down the street just as Jerrod Petrie came running out of the front of the house. He was only wearing his pants and the red bra.

Nick ducked down in his seat, but I could tell he was laughing too.

"You're right," I said. "I'm going to have to burn that bra and panty set."

"We should also probably get a new car. I doubt he was able to see my plates, but there aren't a lot of people who drive this kind of truck and park at the municipal building."

I looked at the clock. It was going on noon. "Do you still have time for sex?"

"Sex first. Car later."

Chapter Fourteen

I WAS PRETTY much toast for the rest of the day, but to be fair, I had gotten up early and I'd crossed another case off my list. Other than the black eyes and perpetual wedding disasters, I was having a pretty good week.

I was lying flat on my back in the middle of the bed, and I raised my head to look down at myself and then promptly dropped my head back on my pillow. I still wore one sock, and my sweater was around my neck. The good news was my face didn't hurt anymore, but I was mostly numb everywhere, so I wasn't sure if that was a good thing.

I was pretty useless after sex. It had the opposite effect on Nick. He got up, showered, and was dressed before I'd managed to come out of my stupor. He kissed me on the forehead and was off to buy a new car and salvage some of his workday.

I halfway lifted my arm off the bed to tell him goodbye.

I must've dozed for a little while, because I was startled awake by the buzzing of my phone and the fact that I was freezing cold. I curled the comforter around me as I turned toward the nightstand and reached for my phone. I was nice and cozy in the cocoon I'd made for myself.

"'Lo," I answered.

"I've got two things to tell you," Rosemarie said.

"Are they good things?"

She was silent. "It depends on if you're a glass half-empty or glass half-full kind of person."

"What's the first thing?" I asked.

"I've got a little impromptu bachelorette dinner planned for tonight. I found a band that can play at the reception, so I thought it'd be a good idea to check them out in person. We can eat, drink, and listen to great music."

"Okay…" The last thing I wanted to do was get dressed and lose my sex buzz, but Rosemarie had gone to the trouble of lining everything up, so I was going. "That doesn't sound so bad. What's the second thing?"

"You left your van at the agency, so I figured I'd park my car there and drive the van to pick everyone up. Like a designated chauffer."

"How were you going to drive the van without keys?" I asked.

"Oh, I've got a set of keys. Scarlet gave them to me just after you got it. I think everyone has keys. She said it was in case of emergency."

"Huh," I said. Good to know in case the van ever went missing. "What else happened?"

"I got in the van and was heading toward the courthouse to pick up Kate when I saw this movement in my rearview mirror. At first I thought it was a bear or maybe Cujo and it was barreling straight toward me and screaming a little. Scared the crap out of me. So I swerved because I thought I was about to be eaten and I accidentally hit some trashcans. And a traffic cone. But the policeman directing traffic jumped out of the way just in time."

I closed my eyes, and figured I'd be getting a call from Nick once the word got back to him that Black Betty was trying to maim officers. It's not like she was hard to pick out in a lineup.

"What happened to Cujo?" I asked.

"It was just Scarlet wrapped up in that stupid fur coat. She went into hiding after that incident at the pawn shop and it was the only place she could think of to go on short notice. I guess she was cold and a little hungry, which explained all the growling."

"How bad is the damage?" I asked.

"On a scale of one to ten, I'd say it's a two. And that officer's handprints should come right off."

"What time are you picking me up?" I asked.

"I've got a couple more stops to make and then we'll head your way. Maybe an hour."

"That'll work."

I disconnected and thought about staying in my cocoon and not going anywhere, but I tossed off the covers and padded my way to the bathroom for a shower and more than just emergency makeup. I needed my RuPaul makeup case. There was nothing that stuff couldn't hide.

It was a good thing I didn't have long hair anymore because my makeup took up almost the whole hour. But the time I was finished, my black eyes were covered and my nose was only slightly swollen. My face was pretty much shellacked, and I was afraid if I smiled too much it might crack.

The only thing I couldn't fix was the bloodshot eyes, so I added false eyelashes and bright red lipstick so I was symmetrically color coordinated.

"I can't work miracles," I said to my reflection.

Since we were going out on the town I decided to pull out the big guns. I had a pair of faux leather *Spanx* leggings that were the best thing since sliced bread. They made me look hot and thin, but also allowed me to eat all the dessert I wanted. It wasn't pretty when they came off, but sometimes you had to make sacrifices for beauty. I put on a tight red sweater and plumped up my cleavage. I didn't have to plump it much. The girls were looking good all on their own. I finished off my look with a pair of impractical Louboutin booties that would have my feet screaming by the end of the night.

I was bachelorette ready. Whatever that meant. There was no telling with Rosemarie.

The buzzer for the front gate sounded just as I made my way down the stairs. I opened the gate and watched as the headlights came closer to the house. I had a fur-lined black cape I never got a chance to wear, so I tossed it over my shoulder, grabbed my purse and was out the door.

Rosemarie screeched to a stop right in front of me and the side door of the van opened. I saw Scarlet's face just before a bag was tossed over my head and I was yanked into the van.

"What the hell?" I tried to yell, but the bass was pumping too loud for anyone to hear me.

The tires squealed and the van shot off like a rocket, and I fell back into one of the seats.

"Who's ready to par-tay?" Rosemarie asked. Her voice was amplified through a mic. Between the music and all the hoots and hollers in answer to Rosemarie's question, I was in my own personal kind of hell. I was not a party animal. I was a 'sit against the wall and watch other people be party animals' kind of person.

All of a sudden, the bag was jerked off my head and a bright light was flashed in my eyes.

"Are you ready?" Scarlet asked.

"Ready for what?"

"I said, are you ready?" she yelled, sounding like a drill sergeant.

I was trying to look around to see who all was in the van, but the bright light had limited my vision. All I could hear was the bass and Rosemarie singing show tunes into the mic, and occasionally giving a play-by-play of what was happening on the streets like we were on one of those Hollywood tour buses.

"Maybe you should give her a little space," I heard my mother say. "She's got that little wrinkle between her brow that she gets whenever she's irritated."

"I know it well," my sister said. "Usually when the wrinkle appears her fists start flying. She chipped one of my teeth once."

"No, I didn't," I said. "You tripped and bumped your chin against the bar."

"Because you punched me," she said.

"Can someone turn that down?" I asked. "I can't hear myself think."

"That's the point," Scarlet said. "We've got to keep you confused and disoriented. Spy school 101."

"This is supposed to be my bachelorette party."

"Huh," she said. "I hadn't heard anything about that. All I heard was detain and blindfold."

"Where are we going?" I asked as loudly as I could.

"It's a surprise," Kate said from the front seat. "All I know is that I'm getting drunk. Loosen up a little. You're getting married."

I hadn't had a chance to tell her we no longer had a preacher to marry us. In fact, I'd barely spoken to Kate all week, but from the few things she had said, I was guessing court was a nightmare.

"How come you look like one of those mannequins?" Scarlet asked, flashing the light in my face again.

I grabbed the light out of her hand and turned it off. "Because I have two black eyes and I had to practically use varnish to cover it up. No thanks to you."

"Me?" Scarlet asked. "You don't have the sense that God gave a jackrabbit. Can't you tell when someone is getting skittish and about to start throwing punches? It's like you haven't learned anything I've taught you."

It turns out I had some unresolved anger toward Aunt Scarlet. I was about to get married and I looked like the Corpse Bride.

"Well you certainly didn't teach me to swing banjos at people or pull out your weapon like Dirty Harry and wave it around. I'm not a cop. I can't do that stuff."

"That's true," Kate said. "We're not allowed to do that stuff."

"Well, thank goodness you're not a cop," Scarlet said. "You'd be a terrible cop. Cops are too friendly now. I miss the old days. Like Eliot Ness. You think Eliot Ness would give two hoots if he was supposed to arrest a criminal or not? You don't have the instinct. The gut always knows. Besides, I made a citizen's arrest. I can do that."

"Right, which is why you whacked her and ran out the door before the cops could show up," I said.

"I had an appointment," Scarlet said.

I knew something was different about Scarlet, but things had been too confusing once I'd gotten in the van to piece it together.

"What happened to your hair?" I asked.

"All those extensions got too heavy. I could barely hold my head up, and when I ran out of that pawn shop I snagged it on one of those planter hooks they attach to the light posts. Thought I'd ripped the whole thing plum off my head. Hurt like the dickens."

That didn't explain why she looked like she'd stolen Sharon Osbourne's hair. It was fire-engine-red and sticking out in all directions.

"This here's a wig," she said, pulling off the hair to reveal a skull cap underneath. "I've decided this is the way to go. Then I can wear different hair every day. It's like changing your underpants, only people can see it."

"I haven't heard this story about banjos and black eyes," Kate said from the front. "Am I going to get sued for something?"

"It's still up in the air," I said. "But be glad Scarlet doesn't work for you or the answer to that question might be a little different."

"I don't work for anyone," Scarlet said. "I'm like my own government. When you get to be my age you realize nobody has a lick a sense and that you don't really care about what people think or why they want to talk about themselves so much. When it comes down to it, people are pretty boring. Just do your own thing, man, and have fun."

"Spoken like a true stoner," Phoebe said, laughing.

My mother gasped and narrowed her eyes at Scarlet. "Were those your rolling papers in my bathroom?"

Scarlet put her hair back on and finally took a seat. "I don't know what you're talking about, Phyllis. You accusing me of something?"

"Who wants booze?" Rosemarie yelled into the mic, and everyone but me raised their hands in the air and made excited hoots and hollers.

"Are we there yet?" my mother asked. "I didn't get a chance to eat today. Do you think they have fondue?"

"It's not 1977," Aunt Scarlet said. "Nobody has fondue. What Addison needs is some oysters. That'll get those ovaries in good shape for the wedding night. You've got to prep for a good wedding night. Like stretching. Otherwise you tap out too soon and no one has fun. I should write a book. I could help a lot of people with my knowledge."

"Yeah, it'd be a real service to the community," my mother said.

"We're here," Rosemarie sang into the mic.

I looked out the window as we pulled into the parking lot of a huge wooden barn. There was a huge flashing sign that said Bucking Bronco's and a picture of a cowboy roping a steer next to it.

"Is this a steak house?" my mother asked.

"Yep, they serve beef all right," Scarlet said. "Let's get this party started."

"I thought we were checking out a band," I said to Rosemarie.

"We are," she said. "They come on at ten o'clock after the main entertainment."

She parked the van in two parking spots and we all filed out. It wasn't until I had two feet on the ground and looked around at our ragtag group that I realized Lucy was with us. It's like she'd just appeared out of nowhere.

"We need a group picture," my mother said. "Something to commemorate this night."

Kate leaned over and whispered, "I'm not sure it's a good idea to have any proof this night ever happened."

I wasn't familiar with Bucking Bronco's. I didn't even know what city we were in. But I knew without a doubt that I needed to stay sober as a judge. We all followed Rosemarie to the entrance where the bouncer was checking IDs. He was a huge black man with a bald head and muscles that didn't fit inside his sleeves. And he took one look at us, and a grin split his face from ear to ear.

He ushered us all in without looking at a single ID, and Scarlet gave him a complicated handshake as she walked by.

"That's what I'm talking about," she said as I came up

beside her. "I've got a weakness for bald black men. You might be minus one before the night is over."

I sighed. It was going to be a long night.

Chapter Fifteen

ROSEMARIE CHECKED us in with the hostess and she showed us to the coat check area. It was then I really got a good look at everyone, and I wondered how we all existed on the same planet, much less in the same group.

My mother was wearing red harem pants and a matching top with sheer sleeves. Her hair was piled up on top of her head and giant gold earrings dangled from her ears. My sister was in her standard torn jeans and she wore a crazy top that had a lot of zippers and angles, and managed to look incredibly sexy at the same time.

Then there was Lucy. She stood off to the side, apart from the group, and she was scanning the crowd. She wore black leather pants—the real kind—and I had a feeling there was no stretch in them like mine. She also wore a black leather top that zipped up the back. I wondered who zipped it for her. Maybe she was married. Maybe she lived in a coven. I had absolutely no idea. But I was willing to bet she was carrying at least six different weapons.

Kate was dressed like Kate always dressed. She wore the black slacks she'd had on in court and a pinstriped, button-up blouse. Her only effort to look more relaxed was that she wasn't wearing the matching suit coat. Then there was Scarlet with her Sharon Osbourne hair and a white jump-suit with a rhinestone belt hanging low on her hips. The look might have looked sexy on someone sixty years younger who didn't have the body of a soup chicken, but she looked like a cross between old Elvis and Evel Knievel.

Rosemarie was always a wildcard. She liked to dress for specific occasions, and I guess since we were at Bucking Bronco's, she figured slutty cowgirl was the way to go. All I could think was that she must be freezing in her rhine-stone boots. She wore a mini denim skirt that barely covered her backside, and a halter top made of western plaid with the little pearl buttons up the front. Only Rose-marie was generous in the bosom area, so her buttons weren't buttoned.

"Good Lord," Scarlet said, looking at Rosemarie. "I didn't know it was a full moon tonight."

The hostess came back to us and looked a little wild-eyed as she tried to figure out who was best to make eye contact with. And then she told us to follow her. The music was louder, and the place smelled of beer, sweat, and meat. I swallowed and tried to breathe through my mouth, but sweat broke out on my forehead. I was hoping it didn't cause streams of makeup to pour from my face.

"We're VIPs," my mother said excitedly, clapping her hands.

"And we're right by the Bucking Bronco," Scarlet said. "I've been known to go eight seconds a time or two in my day. How do you think my fourth husband died?"

Our VIP section was cordoned off with a red velvet rope and it was right in front of the stage. The stage was divided into three sections and big red curtains were down over each one, so no one could see what was going on behind the scenes. Muscled waiters wearing Wranglers, no shirts, and cowboy hats carried trays filled with beer and steaks.

I felt the gorge rise in my throat again and swallowed rapidly. Our table was shaped like a horseshoe so none of the chairs had their backs to the stage. Before I knew what was happening a sash was put over my head and Rosemarie was pinning a tiara to my head. They put me right in the center of the horseshoe.

I didn't like surprises. I liked being in control. I also liked things that smelled good and cleanliness, but I was over-ruled. Before I knew what was happening shots were brought to the table and I watched in fascination as everyone did the first one, just to take the edge off. Even Lucy. I was guessing Rosemarie forgot she was going to be the designated chauffeur because she did her shot and then ordered another round.

It wasn't too long before I was sitting at the table by myself with a glass of water and a pounding headache. Scarlet had disappeared, and I had a feeling she was sizing up the bouncer. And Rosemarie was riding the Bronco like she'd been doing it her whole life. And everyone was getting a free show because straddling a bronco in a tiny denim skirt doesn't leave a lot of room for modesty.

My phone buzzed and I picked up on the first ring when I saw it was Savage.

"Please tell me you need me for something," I said.

"That sounds like a trap," he said. "Is the wedding still on?"

"I'm at my bachelorette party."

"That explains all the 'yee-haws' I'm hearing in the background."

"It's hard to explain," I said.

"It almost always is with you. I'm heading to Whiskey Bayou tomorrow. Want to go with me?"

"I'm assuming it's not just a casual visit because you love the area," I said.

"I need to ask Pastor Charles some questions. I figured it's better to surprise him than give him a heads-up his cover's been blown."

"Sure, my calendar is clear in the morning."

The lights started flashing over the stage areas, and the curtains on the smaller stage on the right opened up, revealing the band.

"Woooooooooooo!" Rosemarie yelled right next to my ear. She'd snuck up on me. "That's them," she said, whacking me on the shoulder. "That's your wedding band!"

"Don't you dare laugh," I told Savage. I put a finger in my other ear so I could hear him.

"I wouldn't dream of it," he said. "I'll pick you up at the office."

I hung up the phone and looked up at Rosemarie. She was still on her feet cheering on the band and my mother was on the other side of her.

"I didn't think you were ever getting off that bronco," I told her.

"Me either," she said. She'd picked up a pink cowboy hat somewhere along the way and she scooted it back so she could see me better. "My thighs kept sticking to the saddle and I couldn't get off. They had to bring over some talcum powder from the pool table and throw it between my legs. It looks like I've been snorting cocaine through my vagina down there."

I willed myself not to look, but I was sitting almost at eye level. She was right. There was a lot of powder on those thighs. It was about that time that the band went into a raucous version of "Bump and Grind" by R. Kelly, and the curtains hiding the other two stages opened to screams all around the room.

A line of men wearing nothing but chaps and cowboy hats walked onto the stage and began to dance. Rosemarie was screaming and pounding on my shoulder, and my mother was standing on a chair. All the waiters who'd been delivering drinks had put down their trays and now they were dancing in the aisles.

"I'm really impressed by the choreography," Kate said, taking the seat beside me.

"That's what you're impressed by?" I asked.

Her shirt was mussed and unbuttoned and she had the glassy-eyed stare of someone who'd had too much to drink. I goggled as she took another shot of tequila that was on the table and then sucked on a lime.

"What's going on?" I asked, nudging her as she shoved some dollar bills into our dancing waiter's jockstrap.

"I'm thinking about selling the agency," she said.

I sat up straight at this bit of news and tried to wave away the gyrating flesh that was entirely too close to my face, but he was persistent since Kate was still holding money in her hand.

I grabbed it from her and shoved it into his pants and said, "Go away." And he shrugged and moved on to the next table of women.

"What do you mean you're thinking of selling? I thought you loved the agency."

Kate shrugged and slugged down another shot of tequila. "I'm just tired of it all. I built it up and it's all mine. And don't get me wrong, the money is nice. But I'm not sure it's worth dealing with the bullshit. Like this trial this week. These complete scumbags get on the stand and try to shred my reputation, and they don't care. They're scumbags. And that's who we deal with. Every day. All day. It'll never change."

"Well," I said. "It's not like that's a surprise. That's why people hire us. To catch the scumbags red-handed."

"I think I just need a change of pace. A change of scenery. Everything is under a lot of strain. And I mean everything."

A few months back Kate had discovered her husband, Mike, had a gambling addiction. From what I could tell, they'd both been working on their marriage, but Kate was pretty closed-lipped about her personal life. Even with me.

"What does your gut tell you?" I asked.

She took a deep breath and then let it out and said in a rush, "That if our marriage is going to survive then we need a change. I need to sell the agency. Mike needs to transfer to another department or retire altogether. And we need to leave here and start over."

It felt like I'd been kicked in the gut. Kate had been my best friend since we were in diapers. I'd never known a life without her in it.

"What does Mike say?" I asked.

She sniffled and I could see tears gather in the corners of her eyes. Kate *never* cried. "He says he'll do whatever it takes to make it work."

"Then that's what you've got to do," I said. I knew I wouldn't be able to hold back the tears when Kate started crying. I was a sympathetic crier. We hugged each other and cried through at least two of the numbers.

"The band is pretty good," Kate finally said.

"Yeah," I agreed. "I wonder if the strippers come with them? I'm not sure Whiskey Bayou is ready for that kind of reception."

"If you're going to go out," she said, "go out with a bang. Kind of like Scarlet did when she was shipped off to France. No one has ever forgotten her."

Boy, was that the truth.

"We have a good tribe," I said. "Weird. But good. Where's Lucy? I was surprised to see her with us."

"She's probably checking on some things. She owns this place. It's how we got the VIP seats."

My mouth dropped open. "Someday you're going to have to tell me about Lucy."

"Not much to tell," Kate said. "She's worked for me almost since the beginning. Savage introduced us."

"You've known Savage that long? Why didn't you tell me?"

"Why would I? We worked together from time to time. It wasn't a big deal. And he never seemed like your type. Besides, he and Lucy were dating at the time. That would've been weird."

"What?" I asked. I felt like I'd just fallen into the rabbit hole. "How could I not know these things?"

"There's probably a lot you don't know," she said, shrugging. "How am I supposed to know what you do and don't know?"

"How did she and Savage meet?"

"How am I supposed to know? I've never asked them. I assume they met on the job."

"Aha!" I said. "I knew she wasn't just a secretary."

"Of course not," Kate said. "Why would I hire just a secretary? She speaks five languages and she handles our more delicate international cases."

"Huh," I said. "Who knew?"

"Well, I did," Kate said. "I hired her. She's my first choice as a buyer for the agency."

"Why'd she come to work for you?"

"Because I pay her a hell of a lot more money than she ever made working for the government. Lucy's quite the entrepreneur. She's got businesses like this all over Georgia."

I was speechless. Well, almost speechless. "No wonder Savage wouldn't answer me when I asked if he'd ever had a long-term girlfriend."

"I don't mean to change the subject," Kate said. "But you should probably see to Scarlet. It'd be embarrassing if Lucy had to ban us from this place."

"I can't see us spending a lot of time here," I said. "But you're probably right."

I watched as Scarlet shoved a woman off a table and climbed up in her place. She was impossible to miss in the white Elvis suit and red wig. Scarlet started to dance and wave her money in the air. And she was just about to step onto the stage when the woman she'd knocked over hopped up from the floor and reached for Scarlet.

"That's my cue," I said, coming to my feet. But it was too late. I got there just in time to see the red wig flying onto the stage. One of the dancers stepped on it and screamed at a decibel level that would've made dogs cry. It was pretty much chaos after that.

Chapter Sixteen

THURSDAY

I woke up feeling much better than I had the day before. My face was more flexible and I could use a myriad of facial expressions. The bad news was my black eyes were a lovely shade of purple and black.

Nick had sent me a text saying he'd had a breakthrough on his case, and that his grandfather couldn't wait for the wedding. He was the one person in Nick's family that actually liked me. He'd also sent me a picture of the new Porsche Cayenne he'd bought after he'd traded in his truck. I shook my head. That wouldn't stick out at all in a parking lot full of beat-up cop cars.

I was getting a late start since it had been well after one in the morning by the time I'd gotten most everyone home. Lucy had opted to stay at the club and oversee the clean-up, and then I'd made the drive to Whiskey Bayou to drop off

Kate, my mom, and Phoebe. Scarlet was persona non grata in my mom's house and Rosemarie had passed out to the point I couldn't wake her up, so I'd hauled them both home with me.

I showered and dressed, and decided to save my RuPaul makeup kit for the wedding day. The day called for simple, because after the week I'd had, I was stick-a-fork-in-me done, so I wore jeans, a sweatshirt I'd had since college that was so soft and threadbare I was always afraid one more wash would be the end of it, and a pair of black Uggs.

I figured my houseguests would be out of it for most of the morning, so I crept downstairs to the kitchen to start my coffee, but there was already a pot brewing. Rosemarie was up and dressed in a yellow velour sweat suit, and she only looked a little worse for wear as she made fried egg sandwiches.

"You're up bright and early," I said.

"Habit," she said. "And I don't get hangovers."

"Must be nice."

"It's come in handy a time or two. I looked in on Scarlet. Had to check her pulse to make sure she was still breathing. She had her wig off and her mouth was open. Thought she was dead."

"Hopefully she'll be out a while. She partied pretty hard."

"It was definitely a night to remember. I called in a sub for the rest of the week," she said. "This wedding business will take it out of you, and I'm not as young as I used to be."

"I haven't thanked you for all you've done," I said, heading to the coffee pot. I got my insulated to-go cup down from the cabinet and filled it to the rim. Cream and sugar wasn't in the cards for today.

"Oh, no need to thank me," she said. "That's what friends do. And besides, this has made me realize that I could do this for a living. I've had much more fun this week than I've had teaching, that's for sure. Kids have changed. They're disrespectful and their parents are nightmares. Being a wedding planner and dealing with bridezillas every day would be a cakewalk compared to dealing with some of those kids."

I kind of saw her point. I'd taught a lot of great kids. But I'd also taught a lot of stinkers, who were the children of even bigger stinkers. I couldn't say that I missed teaching all that much.

"Wow," I said. "That's a huge life change." Everyone was making huge life changes. It felt like parts of my life were being reshaped by high winds and chaos. Kind of like the Bermuda Triangle, only without the death.

She flipped the eggs onto a plate and then handed it to me. I was starving. I hadn't had anything but water since the night before.

"I already have all the contacts," she said. "And I'm always posting those pretend weddings on my Pinterest boards. Lots of people like to follow those so I figured I'd start advertising my services."

"That's a great idea," I said. "You've got a knack for it." I ate my fried egg sandwich in three bites and followed it with coffee. "I hate to eat and run, but I've got to meet Savage this morning. We've got to meet with Pastor Charles."

"Would you mind if I catch a ride with you? Kate's got my keys. She said she'd have Mike drop her off at the agency and she'd drive my car back. Something's up with her. That trial must be wearing on her."

I hmmed noncommittally, thinking about the changes coming in Kate's life. Everyone was moving on, myself included.

"Are you okay?" she asked. "You look kind of green."

"It's my bruises. I didn't get good coverage."

"Are you sure? Because you're really not looking good."

"I'm great," I said, knowing I was absolutely not great. I knew better than to eat something greasy that fast.

I ran to the bathroom and barely made it in time. I immediately felt better and went back upstairs to brush my teeth. My face was still clammy and pale, so I wetted a washrag and washed my face, taking off any remaining remnants of coverage. I didn't care at this point.

When I went back downstairs, Rosemarie was waiting by the door with both our coats and a to-go cup.

"No more coffee for me," I said. "Maybe not ever."

"It's ginger ale," she said. "It'll soothe your stomach."

I put on my coat and then took the cup and put on my sunglasses. I was as ready as I'd ever be, and I was feeling much less excited about the day. I still had one major problem, other than hunting down a drug lord in a town of three thousand people. We still didn't have anyone to marry us.

Savage was already parked in front of the agency in his black Tahoe when we arrived, so I pulled into the space behind him. I was assuming he'd prefer to take his car instead of Black Betty.

"Yikes," he said when I got in the car. "Must've been some bachelorette party."

"I didn't drink at all. Mostly I cried and then had to break up a fight between Scarlet and a lady she pushed off a table."

"Her breakfast didn't agree with her," Rosemarie said. "I told her she should've had a steak last night to tide her over. Bucking Bronco's has the best steak in Georgia."

It was the mention of Bucking Bronco's that reminded me about Lucy. "How come you never mentioned that you and Lucy used to date?"

The corner of Savage's mouth tightened, but that was his only reaction.

"No way," Rosemarie said. "I had no idea."

"You'd have thought with all the strippers there that none of y'all would've had time to talk," Savage said.

"We're women," I said. "We multi-task. Speaking of multi-tasking, did you happen to run that background check I needed?"

I had one open case left, and it was the simple background check he'd volunteered to do for me.

"I already emailed it to Lucy for you," he said.

"I guess you've got her email," I said.

He rolled his eyes, but still didn't give away any information. It was a maddening skill.

"He's good," Rosemarie said.

"I'll get him to break one day."

Savage just smiled and kept driving. "You've got a clear caseload," he said. "Now you can focus on the wedding. You do still want to get married, don't you?"

"How come you get to ask me questions, but you don't answer mine?"

"I save that kind of information for my girlfriends," he said. "The position is open. You didn't answer the question about getting married."

"Damn," Rosemarie whispered. She was leaning forward from the back seat and her head was right between ours.

I sighed and slumped back in my seat. "Thanks for the background check. It's the first time I've ever had a completely clear caseload." And then I thought about the implications of Kate selling the agency. Would I even have a job when all was said and done?

Savage took the exit for Whiskey Bayou and drove straight to the church. Pastor Charles's car was exactly where it had been the last couple of days, but there were no other cars in the lot. Beverly didn't come in until nine.

Savage parked at the back of the lot and we all got out. The sky was gloomy. I was having trouble remembering the last time I saw the sun shine.

"This is like déjá vu," Rosemarie said. "It seems just like yesterday when you were getting married here for the first time."

Savage coughed to cover his laugh, and I gave him the stink eye.

"Thanks for reminding me," I said, shivering beneath my coat. I was almost positive my shivers had everything to do with the weather and not the feeling of impending doom. *Almost.*

"Do you think he's really here?" Rosemarie asked. "This place looks deserted. No cars in the parking lot, and his car hasn't moved in three days. It's like an omen."

It did look rather bleak. "Beverly said he's been in and out. Morning is the best time to catch him. Do you think he'll talk to you?" I asked Savage. The cold must have affected my thinking process because one look at his face made it very clear Savage had no plans to talk to him.

He just smiled at me, like that was going to have any effect on me whatsoever. I mean, sure he had that cute dimple at the corner of his mouth and he was giving me that look he always had right before he wanted to kiss me. But I was an engaged woman, and all that kissing stuff was off the table.

He was nothing more than an incredibly hot, muscle-bound…co-worker. Who had a life I knew absolutely nothing about.

"I don't know what's happening here," Rosemarie said. "But I feel like a dark spirit has descended over this place. It's giving me the chills. I say we go home and you can find a new place to get married." She made the sign of the cross and that gave *me* the chills.

"Stop it," I said. "You're not even Catholic. And this has nothing to do with me getting married. He hired me to do a job, and that's what I'm doing."

"Keep telling yourself that," she said, and crossed herself again.

I was feeling the wedding day pressure and Rosemarie had just hit my last nerve. I launched myself toward her. Savage grabbed the collar of my coat like a puppy, and I almost strangled myself.

"Slow down there, tiger," he said. "Are you sure you want to get married?"

"Stop asking me that," I said, shaking myself loose. "You've got to move past me. I know that you're mildly attracted to me, and on another level, I'm sure I give you a glimpse of the lighter side of this job. I know you're mired in the muck of the horrible things people do to one another on a day-to-day basis. And here I am, like a zoo animal, ready to amuse you when you're bored."

"What you're saying is you're a zoo animal I'm mildly attracted to?" he asked.

"Shut up. You know what I mean." I was starting to get flustered, but I was having trouble closing my mouth. "Plus, you're a fantastic kisser. And I'm not so bad myself, so I see the appeal there." For some reason, I wanted to make sure I didn't take away from the compliment I'd just given him about his kissing, so I reinforced it with a, "Really, you're very good."

"I appreciate that," he said, grinning.

Rosemarie was staring at me wide-eyed, as if I'd lost my mind. Maybe I had.

"You just don't seem like the settling down type," I said against my better judgment. "You're very tempting because you have that bad-boy, rule-breaker vibe. And all the crazy socks are weirdly sexy. And then your body…"

I was talking so fast I was starting to deprive my brain of oxygen. Maybe I'd pass out and by the time I woke up the wedding and anything else I could possibly embarrass myself about would be over.

"I'm just saying that you need a woman who gives you hell," I said. "Everything seems to come easy for you, and that includes women. The second I would've given in to temptation you would've dropped me like a hot rock. And then where would I be?"

"Not standing in single-digit temperatures in a church parking lot," he answered.

"Right," I said, nodding.

Rosemarie looked back and forth between the two of us and crossed herself again.

I rolled my eyes.

"What?" she asked. "I like it. I do it all the time. I saw that demon woman Patty Strobel at the Piggly Wiggly fighting over the last roll of toilet paper to prepare for the big storm. I tell you, she was going to punch Maggie Gerber right in the face. And you know Maggie is older than dirt. She would've disintegrated right there on aisle seven. But I made the sign of the cross and cast out the demon. Patti collapsed right there at Maggie's feet."

"That's because Maggie tased her. She had burn marks right in the center of her chest."

Rosemarie hmmphed and gave me the side eye. "I'd expect that from an unbeliever. Got an explanation for everything."

"Let's just get this over with," I said. "I'm in a crisis. In case y'all haven't realized it, we don't have a preacher to marry us."

"One person's crisis is another's opportunity," Savage said.

"Is that in the Bible?" Rosemarie asked.

Savage just smiled at her, and she unbuttoned her puffy yellow coat and started fanning herself. I couldn't blame her. Savage's smile was dangerous.

"I have a backup plan," I lied. "Everything is going to be just fine. By this time tomorrow I'm going to be a married woman."

Rosemarie flipped open her binder and ran a scarlet-tipped

finger down the page. "Nope," she said. "At this time tomorrow, you'll be getting your eyelashes put on."

I looked at her, horrified. "I already have eyelashes. What are you going to do with my real ones?"

This wasn't the first time she'd made comments about my wedding day preparations that absolutely terrified me.

"Relax," she said. "And I've got you covered. I'm an ordained minister. Got my certificate online last week. I like to have a backup plan. Just in case."

"You'll be an excellent wedding planner," I told her. I was only a little freaked out by the thought of Rosemarie delivering our wedding vows.

"Can we just get this over with and discuss the wedding later?" Savage asked. "If Pastor Charles is here, I've got to arrest him."

"I don't want any part of that," Rosemarie said. "The people in this town will skin you alive for arresting their favorite pastor. There's got to be some rule about that somewhere. Are you allowed to arrest a man of God?"

Savage just stared at her blankly. "He's a murderer."

"I'm just saying, I think it's best if maybe we don't associate with you after the arrest. We want people to still come to the wedding."

Savage took his gun out of its holster and held it down by his side in case anyone passed by. The citizens of Whiskey Bayou weren't exactly known for being subtle.

Rosemarie was right. I was going to be the most hated woman in Whiskey Bayou. Everyone loved Pastor Charles.

I was carrying my Glock concealed, but it wasn't worth the trouble of undoing all my winter gear to get it out. Between Savage and my goose down, I figured I was practically bulletproof.

Rosemarie and I followed Savage up the front steps to the big wooden double doors of the church. My heart hammered in my chest, and I was having a little trouble breathing. The truth was, I hadn't stepped foot in this church since my previous wedding debacle.

Savage put his hand on the heavy iron knob and turned to look at me. "You okay? You look a little green."

"It's the fried egg. I'm all good. Nothing but happy thoughts about this place. I'm getting married. Nothing is going to dampen that excitement."

"That's the spirit," Rosemarie said. "You just put all that other junk out of your mind. The past is in the past. I bet no one even remembers that you got left at the altar, or that they found your fiancé butt naked in the back of your honeymoon limo." She giggled and then put her hand over her mouth. "I've still got the newspaper clippings in my scrapbook. They put those little smiley faces right over his junk and plastered him all over the front page."

Savage's lips twitched and I could see the laughter in the crinkle of his eyes.

"Why are you bringing all this up if you think no one is going to be talking about it?" I asked Rosemarie.

She shrugged. "I don't know. Every time I walk into this church it's the first thing I think about. It's like I can't help myself. You're always good for headlines."

"Are we going to stand out here and reminisce all day?" I asked.

"It's almost worth it," Savage said with a sigh.

He opened the door and slipped into the dim foyer, and Rosemarie and I went in behind him. It took a couple of seconds for my eyes to adjust, but everything looked the same. Marble floors, stained-glass windows, and weird wood-and-iron light fixtures that would instantly impale anyone if they fell from the ceiling.

The doors to the sanctuary were closed, and it felt like the church was completely empty. But a shiver still ran down my spine.

Savage slowly opened the sanctuary doors and we filed onto the red carpeted aisle. I could smell the linseed oil they used to polish the pews and the musty pages of the hymnals. Light filtered in from the floor-to-ceiling, stained-glass windows, and there was a giant cross that hung above the baptismal at the back of the pulpit.

My heart sank, and I looked over at Rosemarie. She crossed herself and held out her fingers in the sign of the cross toward me.

"No offense," she said. "But you have the worst luck."

I wish I could've argued with her, but she was right. There was a body hanging on the cross, and it didn't belong to Jesus.

"Well," Savage said. "Looks like you're going to have to postpone the wedding after all. This is officially a crime scene."

Chapter Seventeen

I THINK it was all just too much, because the next thing I knew, I was flat on my back on the ground and Savage was patting my cheek to wake me up.

"I think I fainted," I said when his face came into focus.

"No kidding. Took ten years off my life."

"That's not Pastor Charles," I said, glancing over at the body.

"I have a hunch it's the guy that answered the phone that day you called looking for Tilda Sweeney. He'd need someone he could trust to help him with some of the details, and Emile Cardonas wouldn't want to leave any loose ends. If Charles and his friend had any contact, Emile would know about it."

I rolled to my side so I could sit up. Rosemarie had taken one of the hymnals and was waving it in front of my face for extra air, but it only made me sneeze, which made my face hurt again.

"You're a mess," Savage said. "I have a theory."

"Listen, Mister," Rosemarie said, getting in Savage's face. "Unless your theory involves getting up there and moving that body out of this church so it's no longer a crime scene, we don't want to hear it. This is our wedding we're talking about. And it's happening whether you want it to or not."

I put my hand on Rosemarie's arm to try and pull her back, but she was fully invested. Savage wasn't really the kind of guy to get overly excited about much. He was like Nick in a lot of ways, which might have been why I'd been a little bit attracted to him. He was still a cop, even beneath his suits, crazy socks, and devil's smile.

All he did was give her a look and she let go of his sleeve. "Sorry about that," she said. "It's the wedding hormones."

His lips twitched and he looked back at me. "They seem to be going around. I need to call in a team and secure the scene. We need to find Pastor Charles."

"Rosemarie and I can look for him while you're stuck here," I said.

"You okay to drive?" He handed me the keys to his Tahoe.

"Just a slight malfunction. I'm good as new."

"Maybe knock on Pastor Charles's front door and see if he answers," Savage said. He stared directly into my eyes and spoke in an unusually even voice. "It's possible there's been a break-in and the front door is already open. It would be perfectly natural and legal for you to go inside and make sure he's okay."

"Right," I said, taking his hand as he helped me off the floor. "Perfectly legal. Come on, Rosemarie. Let's see if we can find a fake preacher."

"I think you should take vitamins," Rosemarie said as we walked around the side of the church to the rectory. "This much added stress isn't good for the body. Look at me, I take my multivitamins every day and I'm fit as a fiddle. I never get sick. And I look healthy. People always talk about my weight, but you don't see me fainting at the drop of a hat or throwing up my eggs.

"Look at you, all scrawny and black-and-blue. You're looking like Anne Hathaway in *Les Mis* after they pulled out her teeth and chopped off her hair. You need some sun and some pie."

"We leave for Tahiti on Sunday," I said. "I'll get more sun and pie than I know what to do with. And sex. And maybe we'll never come back. I could adapt to island life."

"Better watch out," she said. "I heard they have a very active cannibal lifestyle there. They hunt unsuspecting tourists, and before you know it you're being roasted over a spit. Though you might be safe. You don't look very appetizing."

"Thank you," I said. "I think."

The rectory was a simple two-bedroom home made of the same stucco as the church. It was very plain and simple, which I guess was all a single pastor needed. I knocked on the door and then waited to see if anyone would answer.

As expected, no one came to the door, and I listened to see if I could hear anyone moving around inside.

"Should we bust out a window?" Rosemarie asked.

"Probably not," I said, and tried the door knob. It was locked.

I got my phone and called Beverly.

"What's going on?" she said when she answered. "I've already had a hundred phone calls from people asking me what's going on at the church. I was just about to come in."

"I wouldn't bother. The church is going to be shut down for a little while. A body was found on the premises."

She gasped. "Anyone I know?"

"Looks like an out-of-towner," I said.

"Thank God." And then she must have realized what she'd said because she followed up with, "Not that I'm wishing death on anyone. Wow, you have really bad wedding mojo."

"I'm aware," I said. "Is there an extra key to the rectory?"

"Is Pastor Charles in trouble?"

I didn't want to tell her that Pastor Charles was a lying murderer so I just said, "We're making sure he's okay. No one has seen him."

"He keeps an extra key under the little rock in the front flower bed."

I thanked her and hung up, and then bent down to check under the rock. Sure enough, there was a house key sitting there. I unlocked the front door and Rosemarie and I went inside.

"That was easy," I said, looking around.

It was a simple room. White walls and mission-style furniture. There was a crocheted afghan thrown across a worn recliner, and one wall was lined with bookshelves and filled with tattered books. Charles had done a great job of adapting to his new life and making it credible. The fact that he'd been preaching almost every Sunday for ten years blew my mind.

"You know," Rosemarie said. "I always liked his sermons. But I guess it makes sense that I never heard him preaching on the Ten Commandments. The whole murder thing was probably a sticking point."

I grunted and moved to the bookshelf, looking at the tattered volumes. I took out a few of the more used ones and flipped through the pages. Rosemarie was moving between all the framed pictures.

"None of these pictures have him in it," she said.

"Because those are from someone else's life," I said. I went over to the phone and looked through the trashcan next to it. It had been emptied. And then I went through the drawers. They were empty. Where was the clutter? The stuff that showed a person had actually lived there for ten years?

"I'll check the bedroom," Rosemarie said.

I went into the tiny kitchen and opened the refrigerator. Basic stuff—milk, eggs, lunch meat. The freezer was much the same. A stack of TV dinners. I pulled them out and then noticed one of the middle ones wasn't sealed all the way. I pulled back the wrapper and inside the TV dinner were two flash drives.

"Bingo," I said. I put everything back inside the freezer and pocketed the flash drives. There was no telling what was on it.

I joined Rosemarie in the bedroom and she was going through his nightstand drawers.

"Can you believe it?" she asked. "Not even a dirty magazine. How does a man in the prime of his life go without sex for ten years? I've never seen him with a woman or even look like he was interested in anyone. And believe me, I looked. Because that man is hot. I wouldn't have minded being a preacher's wife. Just like Whitney Houston in that movie. I like a good church choir."

"How would you have felt about being a murderer's wife?" I asked.

"I don't know. I was pretty desperate there for a while after my divorce. Anyone would've looked good after Roger."

I looked under his mattress and beneath the bed. Rosemarie was right. There wasn't anything even the least bit naughty. "Maybe when he became a preacher he really found God," I said. "Maybe he's on the up-and-up now and repented. I mean, he's still going to go to jail, but at least he's saved his soul."

I heard a noise from the living room and I froze. Rosemarie's eyes got big and round and her head swiveled back and forth, like she was trying to decide whether to hide in the closet or crawl under the bed. If it was someone we'd known, surely they would've called out instead of trying to be sneaky.

I put my finger up to my lips to signal her to be quiet and moved to the side of the door. The only weapon I could find was a small vase sitting on a secretary. I picked it up and held it over my head. Rosemarie made a little squeak and clapped her hand over her mouth.

My heart was racing a mile a minute and I was going on pure instinct. I brought my hands down just as someone walked through the door. Before I knew it, my wrist was numb and the vase had fallen to the floor.

Savage just stared at me and shook his head. "Aren't you carrying a gun? That wouldn't have been your first choice of weapon?"

"I forgot," I said, completely humiliated. "Besides, it's too hard to get to."

"I'm sure the bad guys love that."

"Except it's just you," I said.

"I can be bad," he said, and then he winked.

"Good Lord," Rosemarie said and fanned herself.

I rolled my eyes. "What's going on?"

"Crime scene team is here. Did you find anything?"

"Yeah, the door was open and we thought there might have been a break-in. So we came in to make sure Pastor Charles was okay."

"That's very neighborly of you," Savage said.

"And while we were looking for his body, I stumbled across these," I said, handing him the flash drives. "They were right in the middle of the floor in plain sight."

"Careless of him to leave them laying around."

We followed Savage back outside, and I noticed the parking lot of the church was full of official-looking vehicles.

"Now what?" I asked.

"Did Charles have any close friends? Anyone he met with on a regular basis?" Savage asked. "If he's not dead, then he's close by. Cardonas is playing with him. He's got eyes on him, and the dead body is a message. He knew Charles would see the body."

I called Beverly again.

"Is he dead? Did you find him? I'm worried sick. My phone's been ringing off the hook."

"We haven't found him yet," I said. "Did Pastor Charles have any close friends? Anyone he met with on a regular basis?"

"He was friendly with everyone, of course." Then she

paused. "Ohmigoodness. I'm using past tense like he's already dead."

"I'm sure he's fine," I lied.

"Well," she continued. "He'd have Bible study with a group of men on Tuesday mornings at the café."

"Do you know if he met with them this week?" I asked.

"No, he had to cancel. He canceled all his appointments for this week or passed them on to Pastor Becky. She's been doing double duty. And she's scheduled to preach on Sunday too. Pastor Charles said he had some personal matters to take care of this week. I didn't pry."

"Can you text me a list of the people he met with most often?" I asked. "Or whoever he was closest to?"

"Sure, I'll do my best."

She hung up and I relayed the conversation to Savage. "You said earlier that you had a theory," I said. "What is it?"

"Oh," he said. "It was a theory about you. Not the case."

I looked at him quizzically. "What theory?"

"You sure you want to know?" he asked.

"Of course. Can't wait to hear it." Savage never got personal. I was expecting him to come up with some cocka-mamie reason Nick and I shouldn't get married.

"Okay," he said. "I think you're pregnant."

Chapter Eighteen

I WAS HAVING AN OUT-OF-BODY EXPERIENCE. That's the only way I could think to describe what I was feeling. If I'd been capable of speech, I would've denied Savage's theory. As it was, I couldn't make my mouth form words.

"Oh," Rosemarie said, and then looked me up and down. "That makes sense. I knew she was acting more nuts than usual, but I figured it was the wedding."

I shook my head no, but I was frozen. I couldn't be pregnant. And then I started doing some math in my head.

"Think about it," Savage said. "You cry at random times for no reason, your sense of smell is heightened and you've been nauseous. And I didn't want to say anything, but your breasts are…" He made a gesture with his hands. "They seem bigger than normal."

"They're huge," Rosemarie said. "They look like they could feed the whole town."

"Ohmigod," I said, looking down. They were right. Scarlet had jinxed me. I was going to have a seven-month baby. "What do I do?"

"Well, I wouldn't tell Nick until after you say 'I do'," Rosemarie said. "Just in case history tries to repeat itself."

"Maybe you should start with a pregnancy test," Savage said. "Just to confirm."

"I can't buy a pregnancy test in Whiskey Bayou," I hissed, looking around just in case there was anyone to overhear. "Everyone in town will know before I walk out the door with it."

"I can't do it either," Rosemarie said. "Everyone knows I can't have children. They'll assume I'm buying it for Addison."

"You have to do it," I told Savage. It was the first and only time I'd ever seen him completely taken aback.

He had a deer-in-the-headlights look and took a step back. I grabbed his arm. "Please. I've got to know. I can't wait."

"And while you're doing that, I can get some pie," Rosemarie said. "This has been a stressful day. I don't know if we're ready for a baby. I'm looking at a career change."

Savage blew out a breath. He was looking a little pale. "Fine," he said. "Let's go."

I was actually surprised he'd agreed. Now that this was happening, I wasn't sure I wanted to know the outcome.

"Park around the corner," I said. "And then you head to the drugstore. Rosemarie and I will walk over to the cafe. After you go to the drugstore, walk back around the building like you're going to your car and then cut across the alley to head back to the café. They'll be watching to see which direction you go."

"This is way too complicated," he said.

"It's Whiskey Bayou," Rosemarie and I said in unison.

Savage headed toward his Tahoe, and Rosemarie and I walked down the street to the café. It was a silent trip. I think both of us were in shock.

When we walked into the café a roomful of people turned to look at us. It was the morning crowd, plus a few extras who were wanting to know what was happening over at the church.

I was greeted with looks of horror as people took in my black eyes, and then a lot of enthusiastic hellos and mentions of the wedding. Nothing could dampen the potential for an open bar. Everyone was looking forward to the party. It looked like there would be a party whether there was a wedding or not. Now that we were without a location, things were looking grim again.

"We'll figure out something," Rosemarie said, reading my mind. "Even if we have to do the ceremony outdoors. We'll just bundle up good. All that matters is that you're married. One way or another. Especially now," she said out of the side of her mouth and pointed to my stomach.

There was a corner booth available back by the restrooms, so we took a seat and waited for someone to come by and take our order. Two waitresses were bustling about, trying to keep up with refills and getting orders filled. Jolene came out of the kitchen carrying a tray of food and delivered it to a table not far from us. When she was done she headed in our direction.

"Good grief," she said. "What happened to your face?"

"Had a runner," I said. "Just part of the job."

"Huh," she said. "Never happened to Magnum P.I. Going to look like the Corpse Bride come tomorrow night. Hope you got a thick veil."

"She's got drag queen makeup," Rosemarie said. "It's like putting Kilz all over your face. Nothing shows through."

"Good to know," she said. "We're busier than usual this morning. Heard there was a body found over at the church. When I realized you and that sexy FBI hunk were in town I figured you'd know the details. Where is he?"

"Doing FBI stuff," I said. "We don't know much right now. All I can tell you is it's not Pastor Charles or anyone else local."

Her lips pinched tight and she turned our coffee mugs over, filling them up with the pot she carried. I turned a third one over and had her fill that one for Savage.

"Well, that's good news at least," she said.

"Has anyone seen Pastor Charles?" I asked.

"I put the word out like you asked," she said. "Mitzi Gerbauch said she thought she saw him driving a maroon Buick yesterday afternoon. She thought it was weird because she'd never seen the car before."

I figured Charles had spent a good part of his life in hiding. He was probably pretty good at disappearing when he wanted to and moving under the cover of darkness.

"Y'all want anything to eat?" she asked.

Now that she mentioned it, my stomach was pretty empty after the egg incident.

"I'll have a full breakfast," I said. "Eggs scrambled. And apple pie instead of the pancakes."

"I'll have the same," Rosemarie said. "And some antacids."

Jolene headed back toward the kitchen, and I watched as Savage came through the door. You'd never know by looking at him what he'd just been doing. He looked calm, cool, and totally in control.

He made eye contact and headed toward us. Instead of sliding into the booth he grabbed an empty chair and pulled it up to the end of the table.

"Please never ask me to do that again," Savage said.

"I can't imagine there'd be more than one occasion for it," I said. "Did you get it?"

"It's in my pocket. I didn't want to carry the bag in."

"That's smart," Rosemarie whispered. "I can see why you've excelled in the FBI."

"Just drop it in my purse." I held my bag open underneath the table and Savage dropped it inside. Then I excused myself and headed to the bathroom.

I'd had a pregnancy scare once before, so I was experienced at test-taking. Once I'd finished my business, I put the test back in the bag and shoved it in my purse. And then I washed my hands and went back to the table. My heart was hammering in my chest like a jackrabbit.

"Well?" Rosemarie asked.

"I've got to wait five minutes," I said. "It's in my bag. Did you order?" I asked Savage.

"Pie," he said. "It's definitely a pie kind of day."

I smiled. It was good to know I could rattle Savage about something.

"Thanks for doing that, by the way," I said. "That goes above and beyond friendship."

"Yeah, well," he said. "I've got a sister. I recognize the signs well. I hope everything works out for you."

There was something in his voice that caught my attention, but I couldn't interpret it. I was having trouble focusing. All I wanted to do was check the results. I looked at the timer I'd set on my phone. Two minutes left.

Savage checked his phone. "It looks like there was ID on the victim," he said. "Probably a fake if he's an associate of Charles. But we'll run his prints. I'm willing to bet he's already in the system. They grabbed prints from the rectory too and should be able to confirm that Charles and Carlos Rodriguez are one and the same."

"What about the flash drives?" I asked.

"Agent Scott just looked at the first one. It's an address book with current names and location of cartel members. It wasn't password protected. We don't know about the second one yet."

"So basically we have two murderers on the loose," I said. "Jolene told me Pastor Charles was seen driving a maroon Buick. Could belong to the victim from the church."

"I'll check it out," he said. It's not your problem. It's in the FBI's hands now. You can still get married with a clear caseload."

Jolene came out of the kitchen with another tray and all our food stacked up, and she slid plates in front of us with practiced ease. She filled our cups, winked at Savage, and then took off again.

I checked my phone again, butterflies racing in my stomach, and then I dug into the pie. Sometimes you needed dessert first, and this was one of those times.

"I can't stand it anymore," Rosemarie said. "It's like how they always cut to commercial right before he gives the rose on *The Bachelor*."

I finished my pie and then saw my timer had run out. It was the moment of truth. I opened my bag and rummaged inside the little paper bag where I'd dropped the test. And I looked at the results.

"It's positive," I said softly. And then I looked at Savage and Rosemarie.

Rosemarie burst into noisy tears and grabbed a bunch of napkins from the dispenser. "I'm so happy," she said, sobbing into the napkins. "I've got to go compose myself." She scooted out of the booth and ran to the bathroom, leaving me alone with Savage.

"Congratulations," he said.

I kind of wanted to cry myself. Nick was going to freak out. We hadn't even really talked about having kids. At least not seriously. It was always one of those later down the road conversations.

"Thanks. I'm kind of numb."

"It's definitely an adjustment," he said.

"What's going on with you?" I asked. "I mean, really. I thought you were taking time off this week, but you've been all over this case. You just seem…different."

He sighed and took a bite of pie, choosing his words, I hoped, instead of choosing not to answer personal questions.

"I needed some time off to think," he said. "I've been offered a job heading up a special task force. I'd be in charge of the FBI field office, but I'd also be working closely with the Bureau of Indian Affairs. There are lots of drugs and other things passing through the reservation, but because of the laws it's not easy to stop it. It would definitely be new and exciting. And a step in the right direction career-wise."

"That's great," I said. "But?"

"But I'd have to relocate to South Dakota."

"Oh, wow," I said. "That's far. What's stopping you?"

He looked at me for a long time and then finally said, "Nothing anymore. I've decided to take the job."

I needed some alone time after the morning I'd had, so once we were back at the agency I got in the van and drove to Tybee Island. I parked on the beach and watched the waves come in.

I had no idea how to tell Nick I was pregnant. Would he be angry? We were just getting started. Just figuring things out. And now we were going to bring a baby into the fold. What was I going to do with my career? I couldn't go getting punched in the face or falling out of trees nine months pregnant.

Everything was changing too fast, and I was completely overwhelmed. I had a good, long cry and then I fell asleep.

When I woke up it was getting dark and a police officer was shining his light in my face through the window. We both jumped. I guess he'd thought I was dead and I surprised him when I moved.

I assured him everything was okay, and that the black eyes were nothing to be concerned about. And then I drove back home. There was nothing else I could do but wake up the next morning and hope that I was married by the end of the day.

Chapter Nineteen

FRIDAY

I knew something was weird before I opened my eyes the next morning. I laid in the dark with my eyes closed, trying to use my other senses and evaluate the situation.

I remembered going to bed the night before and Nick coming in sometime later. He'd been excited because they'd been able to get warrants and there were a lot of very angry rich people about to have their lives turned upside down. The neighbor's security cameras had proved helpful and it looked like a professional team had been hired to kill the Haywoods. Nick had been confident that between the pressure from his grandfather and what was being discovered during the investigation, that someone would eventually go down for murder.

Nick had been pretty revved up with the news and in the mood to fool around, but I'd pretended to be too sleepy because all I could think about was the baby. I was afraid if I opened my eyes he'd somehow know.

He'd left before the sun had come up and told me he had to wrap up some things before the wedding, and that he'd meet me at the church. I was perfectly okay with this. The more time I had to avoid the matter at hand, the better.

"I'll pick up the rings," he said on the way out.

I knew Nick was gone, but it still felt like I wasn't alone. I cracked open an eye and screeched when I saw Scarlet's face, barely an inch from mine.

"Holy cow," I said, grabbing my chest. "You scared me to death."

"I've actually scared a man to death before," she said. "You're okay. Time to get up. It's your wedding day."

"I'm not getting married until tonight."

"Have you seen yourself? It might take all day to get you in working order. You're not married yet. You can't just give up on yourself. That comes a few years down the road."

"Good to know," I said.

"Come on. I made us appointments at the spa. Chermaine has cleared her calendar for this fiasco."

I looked up and saw Scarlet was wearing a different wig today. It was a black, chin-length bob.

"I thought you weren't coming to the wedding."

"I'm not," she said. "I've got to hit the road. The popo's suggestions I talk to them aren't so much suggestions anymore as they are orders. I don't like taking orders. But I've got priorities so I figured I'd hit the spa and get the full treatment before I have the car deliver me to the cruise ship. I want to make a good impression. It takes effort to look this good."

"I can imagine," I said.

I was starting to feel queasy, and Scarlet was totally invading my personal space. "Give me a chance to shower and I'll be down in a few minutes.

"Hmmph," she grunted and moved back. "Don't think you're fooling anyone, girl. I know a pregnant woman when I see one. Better get that man in front of the preacher before you tell him, though. A man can be real skittish about pregnancy."

With that bit of advice, she left the bedroom. I wondered briefly how Scarlet had gotten inside the house, then I realized she'd probably never left after the bachelorette party. Knowing Scarlet, she'd riffled through every drawer we had.

I tossed back the covers and got out of bed, and then laid down on the bathroom floor for twenty minutes until the nausea passed.

I was feeling unsettled, and not because of the pregnancy. Savage had told me not to worry about Pastor Charles since the case was in the FBI's territory now, but I wanted closure. It felt like if things were going to end, and they were definitely ending, then it should be with a little more excitement and pizzazz.

I showered and dressed casually in leggings and a loose button-down shirt, and then I went down to meet Scarlet and head to the spa.

She looked me over and shook her head. "You're definitely a Holmes. You've got grit, girl. And average judgement. But you'll always land on your feet, no matter what happens."

We drove to Savannah and I parked Black Betty outside of Chermaine's, and I realized my shoulders were in knots from the tension. I needed to talk to Nick. I hadn't told him about Kate, Rosemarie, Savage or the baby. I was carrying around a whole lot of worry when I should have been sharing my worries with him. Well, at least about the first three. I still wasn't sure how to tell him about the baby.

My tension only intensified when I opened the door to the spa and saw my mother, sister, Kate, and Rosemarie waiting for us. I heard raucous laughter and saw a flash of color out of the corner of my eye, and my mouth dropped open at the sight of Chermaine coming toward me. Her mohawk was spiked to sharp points and bright red, reminding me of a rooster's comb, and she was wearing lots of zippers and buckles. Her nose, eyebrow, and lip were pierced and her lipstick was black.

Right beside her was Suzanne, looking as diva fabulous as ever. Then I realized what I'd completely missed the first time I'd met Chermaine, though her Adam's apple wasn't quite as prominent as Suzanne's. Not that it mattered. She'd worked magic on my hair the last time I'd come to see her. Hard to imagine it had only been a week ago. A lot had happened in a week.

"I love weddings," Chermaine said, handing me a mimosa and a white robe. "As long as they're not my own. Been there, done that."

She and Suzanne looked me over at the same time, and their gasps were almost identical as they took in my black eyes.

Chermaine put her hand to her forehead and said, "What am I supposed to do with this?"

"What are you supposed to do?" Suzanne asked. "What am *I* supposed to do? You're just doing hair. I'm supposed to do makeup."

"I thought you did cakes," I said.

"Suzanne does a little bit of everything, darling, including work miracles. Everyone is going to get the royal treatment today. A full spa experience."

Chermaine went to the front door and locked it. "Everybody take your clothes off and put on a robe."

A girl appeared out of nowhere and started passing out mimosas to the others. I looked at Rosemarie, wide-eyed, not sure what to do without giving my situation away. She took it out of my hand and downed it in one gulp.

"Just juice for her," Rosemarie said. "She's been drinking too much again."

I scowled at Rosemarie, thinking no one would buy that story, but everyone just shrugged and sipped their own.

"Sorry," she whispered. "It was all I could think of."

We were ushered into a changing area, and everyone stripped down to nothing and put their clothes in lockers.

"You look so calm, Addison," my mother said. "If I was in your shoes and it was eight hours until my wedding, and I had no venue, I'd be a basket case."

"A church is just four walls," Scarlet said. "One time I got married jumping out of an airplane. It doesn't matter where you do it, only that it gets done. And the sooner the better."

I rolled my eyes. If Scarlet wasn't careful I wouldn't have to make an announcement about the baby. She'd end up doing it for me.

"Which reminds me," she said. "I've got a wedding gift for you. Since my presence can't be your present, I got you this. Figured I owed you one for the black eyes."

I took the envelope from her instead of retorting with, *"You think?"* which is what I wanted to do. I figured over the last few weeks, Scarlet owed me way more than just "one." There was a single sheet of paper inside the envelope that looked rather old, and when I examined it I realized it was the deed to the whiskey distillery in Whiskey Bayou. And on the line at the bottom was my name and Scarlet's signature.

"I figure it needs to stay in the family. I can't take it with me when I die. I've got good memories of that place. That's why I kept it for so long. If it wasn't for that factory I wouldn't have gotten shipped off to France. And I wouldn't be where I am today."

"I thought you got shipped off to France because of a man," Phoebe said.

"Yeah, Dean Walker. Boy, was he a firecracker in the sack. But so was I, which is why he gave me the factory as a wedding present. We were going to get married after he left his wife, but my daddy shipped me off. I'd already been given the distillery, though, and Dean died from a heart attack a couple weeks later. It's not like I could give it back at that point. So it all worked out."

"A man died," my mother said.

"It's not like I killed him," Scarlet said. "He had the heart attack because his wife would've taken everything in the divorce."

"It's a miracle they let you come back into town at all," my mother said, shaking her head.

"Don't be ridiculous," Scarlet said. "Everyone's too scared of me. And that's right where I want them. I own lots of those buildings in Whiskey Bayou. I just buy 'em up a piece at a time when no one is looking. I've got lots of dummy corporations."

I shook my head in wonder. "Thank you," I told her, not quite sure what I was going to do with a two-hundred-year-old building that was no longer in use. But maybe Nick had an idea.

"Don't just stand there looking slack-jawed, girl. It's catty-corner from the church. Move the ceremony over there. Problem solved."

"Oh," Rosemarie said. "I've got to call all the vendors and the caterer. That's brilliant."

"Now can we get this show on the road?" Scarlet asked. "I've got a car picking me up in a few hours, and I've let myself go recently." She looked at me. "No offense, but I've aged more in the last few weeks hanging out with you than I have in the last fifty years."

My mouth dropped open at that, and I watched as she flounced away, butt naked. Apparently, Scarlet didn't believe in robes.

"I didn't need to see that," Kate said.

"I wish I could say it even phases me anymore," I told her. "I think that week at the nudist colony damaged me permanently."

"Was that a lightning bolt waxed into her pubic hair?"

"Don't ask," I said.

For the next several hours I was massaged, salted, scrubbed, waxed, lotioned, manicured, and pedicured. If I didn't look in the mirror, I'd almost feel normal. I knew things were serious when Suzanne got out the airbrushes.

"I use these on my cakes," she said. "Sometimes life calls for a little airbrushing. Just try not to breathe. This stuff is amazing. And not even tears will make it come off. You'll get at least three days of use out of it before it starts to fade."

"Is that safe?" I asked.

"Do you want black eyes for your wedding?" she asked.

I shook my head.

"Then take a deep breath."

I did what she said. When I was able to open my eyes again I looked like my regular self. I had color in my cheeks and a nice glow. She'd done my whole body to even things out, and she'd even put a little shading around my collarbone and cleavage.

"Little trade secret," she said. "Though you're not needing a lot of help with that cleavage. Nick's a lucky man."

"Because I've got boobs?"

"It doesn't hurt," she said.

An hour later, we were all ready. Everyone still wore their robes except for Scarlet.

"This is my cue to leave," Scarlet said. She was wearing a white sailor suit with navy trim. Her hair was platinum and in a bun on top of her head. "I've got a ship to catch, and I want to butter up the captain while my skin is still plump and soft. In the dark it feels like it belongs to a thirty-year-old."

My mother coughed loudly and Scarlet shot her a glare.

"I'll see you next November," Scarlet said to Rosemarie.

I looked at Rosemarie in question.

"November is the slow month for weddings. I figure I'll take a break and check out what the land down under has to offer."

"You've got your something old, something new?" Scarlet asked me. "Don't buck with tradition. It's bad luck."

I hadn't even thought of that. "Err…no."

"Well, the deed to the distillery can count as something old," she said.

"I've got the something blue," Kate said.

She handed me a long blue velvet box, and I was expecting some kind of jewelry when I opened it. But instead, it was Kate's set of lock-picks. I'd bought them for her the day she'd opened up the agency. They'd been completely impractical, and I hadn't even been able to afford them at the time, but Kate was my best friend and I wanted her to have something to commemorate such a special day. They were sterling silver, and at the end of each one was a blue diamond.

For as long as she'd been sitting behind her desk at the agency, she'd kept them in a framed glass case on her wall. This was the beginning of the end. She was really selling the agency.

I threw my arms around her and hugged her tight. No one else knew what those lock-picks meant, but I did, and that was all that mattered.

"I've got your something borrowed," my mother said. "I know you're a Holmes through and through, but you get your grit from both sides. My grandmother was a spitfire too, and she'd want you to have these."

"I always liked Ruth," Scarlet said. I think it was the first time I'd ever seen her agree with my mother.

My mother handed me a little square box and inside it were pearl earrings. "I didn't give these to you at the last wedding," she said. "I think because I knew it wasn't right. But these are yours now."

I hugged my mom, and quickly put on the earrings. All that was left was the something new.

Rosemarie handed me a gift bag. "You probably want to open that when you're alone. And don't worry. It's new. Don't be discouraged by the bedazzling. It adds to the pleasure. Nick will thank you."

My eyes widened at that, and I was terrified to look inside. It reminded me of the time Rosemarie and I had accidentally gone to a passion party. We'd gotten to know each other real quick after that. I put the bag in my purse to save for later.

Scarlet looked at me like she wanted to say something, but she straightened her spine and cleared her throat. "Well, girl," she said. "Let me know if you have another wedding before I die. I might come to that one."

With that, she turned and made a grand exit to the car that was waiting for her. I knew in her own way she'd miss us. Scarlet just wasn't all that good at showing emotion. Considering the life she'd led, I guess she'd never had the chance to practice.

"Come on, people," Rosemarie said. "Time's ticking."

"Put your dress on," Chermaine said. "We've got to get going. You don't want to be late to your own wedding."

Everyone scattered to get dressed, and I followed Chermaine and Suzanne to the big room where my dress was hanging.

They helped get me get zipped up, and then pinned in my tiara and straightened my veil. Then I turned to look in the mirror. I would have cried, but I was pretty sure the airbrush had clogged up my tear ducts. Despite the disasters at almost every turn, I knew this wedding was the right one. With the right man. It didn't matter if there were no caterers, food trucks, or open bars. If the cake dropped to the ground or if Nina really showed up in overalls. There was nothing that was going to keep me from marrying Nick.

I took a deep breath and went back out to the front. True to her word, my mom was wearing the dress she'd worn at my last wedding. Phoebe was standing beside her in a backless black gown and flip flops. Kate wore the pale-blue, one-shoulder gown she'd tried on at Le Couture. And then there was Rosemarie.

I never saw what gown she'd ended up picking that night in the dress shop. But I was almost positive what she was wearing wasn't it. She was dressed like a Chinese missionary. Or possibly Hillary Clinton. It was a black silk pantsuit that came down to her mid-thigh, with bell sleeves. She'd added a white clerical collar around the neck.

"I hope you don't mind, but a change in position calls for a change in attire. It's important when one is ordained to look the part. Now stop standing around and get in the limo. We're on a schedule, people."

"Let me get something out of the van," I said. I'd hidden the pregnancy test in the glove compartment because I didn't want anyone to accidentally find it in my purse. But I wanted to be able to show Nick. He was the kind of guy who liked proof.

I slung my bag over my shoulder, hiked up my dress and ran out to the van. I opened the passenger side and was about to open the glove box when I heard the familiar sound of a bullet being loaded in the chamber of a gun. When I looked up, cold steel was mere inches from my face.

Chapter Twenty

I WAS ALMOST TOO scared to look up. I didn't move a muscle, but I let my eyes scan up to the person behind the gun.

"Get in," Pastor Charles said. Gone was the kind man I'd known for the past ten years. I could see his former self right there in his eyes. "Tell them you're driving separately. Do it now, or I'll shoot every one of them."

I backed away quickly before the others became too curious and wandered over, and then I got Rosemarie's attention.

"I'm going to drive myself," I said.

"But the limo…"

"I know, but I need a little time alone. To meditate."

"Is that a code word for bailing out?" she asked. "You're not changing your mind, are you? Because the ba—"

She pressed her lips together and pretended to zip them.

"I'm not changing my mind," I promised. "All is good. I just need to be alone for a bit."

She nodded, but she wasn't happy about it, and she got into the back of the limo with the others. I breathed out a sigh of relief and went around to the driver's side. I tried three times to get in, but between my shaking hands and dress, I wasn't having a lot of success.

"Oh, for Pete's sake," Charles said. He put the gun in the passenger seat and then leaned over and hauled me in. Then he took the gun and moved behind me while I got settled.

I looked in the rearview mirror and almost screamed when I saw someone else sitting in one of the passenger seats. Whoever it was, he was very obviously dead. My van had death cooties.

"Who…who's that?" I asked.

"Emile Cardonas. You did exactly what I needed you to do after I hired you, and I was able to hunt him down. I've always been a fan of the garrote. It's not used nearly enough in my estimation."

"It certainly isn't something you'd want to use if you want an open casket," I quipped. Emile's face was a bruised purple and his staring eyes bulged out.

I waited until there was a break in traffic and then pulled out."I hate to break this to you, but I'm kind of the star of the show. People are going to notice if I'm missing."

"Nobody is going to notice anything," he said. "I need a ride to Whiskey Bayou. If I drove back in myself someone would notice. That place is swarming with agents. All I need is a distraction so I can get in and out, and then disappear for a little while."

"Why do you need to go back? Especially if you know they're looking for you?"

"I left a little insurance behind. I had to leave town rather sudden and didn't get to pack for the trip. And for some reason, people are more interested in my whereabouts than usual. I have a feeling I have you to thank for that. I haven't been able to take a crap in that town this week without someone knowing about it."

I wrinkled my nose. That wasn't a pleasant image. I could see the limo a few cars in front of me, but I deliberately stayed back.

"God, you're a pain in the ass," he said.

I gasped at the thought of him cursing, and then remembered he wasn't really a preacher.

"Seriously?" he asked. "Does my language offend you? You were supposed to be a lot dumber. All I asked was one simple thing. If you'd done what you were supposed to I could've drawn Emile out and killed him without all the hassle. As it was, I had people swarming me twenty-four-seven. It was just sheer luck that made it impossible for Emile to get close enough to kill me."

"Well," I said primly. "It sounds like it all worked out for you. You got what you wanted."

"I should've been out of this crap hole, three days ago. But you ruined my plans. Why the hell did you call in the FBI?"

"I didn't do it on purpose," I said. "Besides, this is a mess of your own making. Don't blame me because you were sloppy and your past caught up to you. I wouldn't have kept digging if your 'friend' hadn't screwed up and told me Tilda Sweeney was no longer working at the church. Her picture was right there on the website. I gave the number you put on your reference sheet to a friend at the FBI. It wasn't that hard for them to connect the dots."

Charles clicked his tongue in annoyance. "Gabriel," he said, shaking his head. "He was loyal, but he was never the sharpest knife in the drawer. In the end, he got what he deserved."

"Who's Gabriel?"

"He had a little mishap at the church," Charles said. "It seemed like a punishment that fit the crime."

"Being murdered and hung up on a cross?" I asked.

Charles shrugged. "I've always had a flair for the dramatic. I've missed that about my old life."

"It seems to have come back to you rather quickly," I said dryly. "Why would you kill your friend?"

"Friend is a relative term," he said. "And I needed to make a point. Everyone in the cartel knew Gabriel and I were close at one time. If I was going to take it away from Emile I had to show them I was ruthless. That no one had a free pass. Once those who are loyal to Emile see the tapes I made of his and Gabriel's deaths, they'll know not to challenge me. They'll know I'm back."

"That was the point of this? So you could go back to your old life and take over the cartel?"

"Of course," he said. "I've spent a decade planning this. I purposely kept in touch with Gabriel. I also knew he hadn't been as careful about keeping his location hidden from the cartel and that they were watching him. He came here looking for me last fall to warn me that Emile was looking for me, but I already knew that. I was finally ready for Emile to find me. And the dummy led him right to me.

"It was the only good thing about living in that crap town. I was safer there than living in any big city. People were so up my ass all the time Emile didn't have a chance to make a move, and he didn't have a chance of sneaking up on me without me knowing about it. He knew he'd screwed up after he stopped at the café that day. Jolene asked him too many questions, and she knew what kind of car he was driving. Told him she'd seen him around town and asked who he was visiting. It made him nervous, so he laid low for a while.

"But he came back, just a couple of days here and there. Emile likes to play, but he doesn't have half the brains his brother did. I let him play. Think he was messing with me. He's never known the best time to strike the sword, and this time he waited too long. He could've tried to kill me when he left that picture on my nightstand, but I knew he was there. I made sure the front porch light was out so he could come in without being seen. The dumbass just stood there, and then he left, hoping to scare me."

"Did Emile want to kill you because you turned on his brother?" I asked.

"Hell no," Charles said. "Emile is the one who ratted me out to the cops. I was standing in his way because Frank was grooming me to take more responsibility in the organization. Emile was jealous. So he set me up, and he figured Frank would put a hit out on me while I was in jail. Which is exactly what he did. I just happened to get lucky and take the deal for witness protection before it could play out."

"Nice bunch of friends you have," I said.

"You know what they say," he said. "Keep your friends close and your enemies closer."

"You made a very convincing preacher," I said.

He smiled. "My mother was devout. It wasn't hard to bring it all back."

We took the exit for Whiskey Bayou and he ducked back behind my seat. He was right about the FBI agents. There were unmarked cars parked at the entrance of Main Street with agents inside. There was probably a little added protection with everything that had happened and the fact that an active senator was attending the wedding.

"I haven't made it this far because I don't have patience," he said. "After I heard your wedding had turned into a block party, it was obvious this was the perfect cover for me to slip into town and get the recordings I'd made killing Emile and Gabriel. Once I get it I'll steal a car and go back into hiding until I'm ready to leak the tapes and position myself to take over."

"Sounds easy," I said, rolling my eyes.

Main Street had been blocked off for the festivities and there were people everywhere. I had a view straight down the street, and I waved at the agents as I passed them. I recognized one of them from the crime scene at the church the day before. The whole town was out in force. I had no idea how I was going to get to my own wedding. *If* I made it there at all.

"Go down a couple of blocks and come back toward the back of the church," he said. "I'll get out at the corner and you can be on your way."

"What about Emile?" I asked.

"He's all yours. Dump him or turn him over to the cops. I don't really care."

"You're seriously going to let me go?" I asked.

"Is there a reason I shouldn't?" he asked. "Killing you would be fun. But it would also cause complications for my escape. Maybe I'll come back to finish the job later."

My phone buzzed and I saw it was Rosemarie. "If I don't answer she'll send a SWAT team after me. She's the wedding planner."

"Answer it, but don't be stupid."

"Where am I supposed to park?" I asked as soon as I answered.

"If you'd ridden with us in the limo you wouldn't have that problem," she said. "They dropped us off right at the front of the distillery. The police have all the streets blocked off because there are so many people."

"Well, this is my wedding, and if I have to drive through people to get there, then that's what I'm going to do. Maybe tell Sheriff Rafferty to let me through."

"I think Nick is taking care of it. I don't think the sheriff likes him much."

"That's an understatement. I'll be there in five minutes," I said and hung up.

I drove a ways down like Charles had asked, and then I headed back toward the church and stopped a couple of blocks before the barricades and the crowds started.

"You'll have to get out here," I said. "Any closer and someone might see you."

"It's been a pleasure," he said, and then he was gone.

I turned in my seat, but Emile hadn't magically disappeared. I still had a corpse in my van.

"This is not the time to throw up," I said. "Breathe through your mouth."

I stepped on the gas and hightailed it toward the distillery. I didn't have very long before Charles was going to discover those tapes were missing. And then all hell was going to break loose.

If I hadn't been in a dead panic, I would've spent more time appreciating all the effort that had gone into the wedding. Strands of lights had been hung in the park, and the food and drink trucks had all been parked on the opposite side so as not to hamper anyone's view. It was like New Year's Eve and Fourth of July all rolled into one. The cold didn't seem to matter.

I beeped my horn as I drove toward the crowd, but people weren't as quick to move as I'd have liked them to be. I was really ready to put some space between me and Emile. I finally gave up on the crowd parting in front of me like the Red Sea and put Black Betty into park. I threw open the door and hopped down, ripping my dress in the process.

I started shoving my way through the well-wishers and dialed Savage.

"We've got a problem," I said when he answered.

"I know, I'm at a wedding and the bride hasn't shown up yet."

"Emile Cardova is in my van. Charles killed him, and he held me at gunpoint so I'd drive him here. He couldn't get into town because of the agents everywhere. He's looking for his tapes, and he's going to be pissed when he realizes they're not there."

"Yeah, that's a problem," Savage said. "Where are you?"

"Trying to make my way through the crowd," I said. "I'm coming up on the west side of the church, but there are too many people."

"I'll meet you near the barricade," he said. "I'll send agents to see if they can run him to ground at his house."

I was putting Suzanne's makeup job to the test, because I was sweating bullets. The smell of beer and the food trucks was strong, and I dodged and weaved my way through the crowd. I could see Nick standing at the top of the stairs by the doors, but I didn't see Savage anywhere.

Nick was scanning the crowd like he always did, and he caught sight of me coming toward him. Something on my face must have shown my panic because I saw him reach down for his ankle holster, and then he started running toward me. Thank goodness I was marrying a man who'd come armed to our wedding.

Nick had almost reached me, and about that time, Savage came up from the side and flanked my other side. And then they both ushered me into the side door of the church and past the crime scene tape.

"We should be able to wait it out here undisturbed," Savage said. "They'll either catch him or he'll see the risk and get the hell out of Dodge."

"What's going on?" Nick asked.

I quickly explained what I'd discovered on my drive into Whiskey Bayou. Nick shook his head in disbelief.

"How does this stuff always happen to you?" Nick asked.

"It's not like it's my fault," I said, throwing up my hands. "I was just trying to come to my wedding like everyone else. Savage told me the FBI was taking care of everything."

Nick and I both turned to look at Savage, and he shrugged. "I've learned that things tend to not go according to plan when you're involved. It's why I had the extra agents stationed at all the entry and exit points around Whiskey Bayou."

I narrowed my eyes. "What are you saying? I've already been told by Charles that I'm a pain in the ass."

"Well," Savage said. "He's not wrong."

The sound of gunfire had us all moving for cover behind the pews.

"It sounds like it's coming from the rectory," I said.

"You stay with her," Savage told Nick. And then he looked at me and reached beneath his jacket, handing me his backup weapon. "Just in case."

Savage took off toward the sound of gunfire and Nick moved me toward better cover. There was one of those moments where time seemed to slow to a stop. I heard more gunfire, and it was closer this time. And I just knew.

Fear rushed through me and Nick and I made eye contact. I could tell staying there was the last thing he wanted to do. I shoved at Nick. "Go," I told him. "I can take care of myself. He needs back up. Go!"

I wanted to cry, but there would be time for crying later. I knew in my gut something was wrong. Savage was my friend and he'd also been my partner at times. We wouldn't leave him to face the enemy alone.

Nick nodded and moved off toward one of the side hallways, and I went in the opposite direction. Toward Savage.

I could smell the blood before I found it. The halls were dark, and the only light was from the strings of light outside, sending odd patterns onto the tile. So when my fingers touched wetness, I wasn't a hundred percent sure what it was until I held my fingers up to the light.

"Oh, God," I said, and my voice broke. I crawled through it, not caring that it soaked through my gown. And then I touched a sleeve. Then a hand. A hand that was still warm.

"Savage," I whispered, looking for his wound. It was impossible to find. His front was soaked with blood.

The gunfire had stopped, and the only thing I could hear was my heart pounding in my ears.

"Savage," I said again, but there was no response. I put my fingers against his throat, searching for a pulse, and breathed a shaky sigh of relief when I found one. Barely. We were in the middle of a long hallway, and there was no cover, so I moved behind him and dragged him toward an open classroom door a few feet away.

I'd just gotten my body inside the door and pulled Savage's torso halfway through when someone flipped on all the lights. They were blinding and I couldn't see anything after being in the dark for so long. And then I heard footsteps coming down the hallway.

I had a choice to make. I could sit there and wait for Charles to find me or I could do what he'd least expect. I had nowhere else to go. I was trapped. I squeezed Savage's hand one more time and crawled to the door with the gun in my hand.

The footsteps had come from the right, so I took a deep breath and counted to three. And I slid out into the hallway on my side with the gun pointed at whoever was coming. I was just in time to hear footsteps behind me, and I wondered if I'd made the wrong decision when there were two shots fired over my head. Almost on top of each other. The man running toward me stumbled as the bullets hit him, and then he came forward a few more feet when another bullet hit his chest.

Charles stared at me out of shocked, glassy eyes, and he tried to lift the gun in his hand, but another shot was fired that dropped him to the ground. Someone leapt over me and made sure Charles was dead, kicking the gun out of his reach for good measure. I met his gaze, thinking how close he'd come to death. How close we'd both come. His chest was heaving, and he was saying something, but I couldn't hear anything but the blood rushing in my ears.

"Addison," Nick said. "Addison," he said again and knelt beside me. "Are you all right? You're not hit, are you?" He was looking at the blood that soaked my dress.

I shook my head. "No, it's Savage's."

I shook my head and real time seemed to come rushing back. I crawled back over to where Savage lay. More footsteps were running toward us, but Nick had already moved into action. He stripped off his tuxedo jacket and put pressure on the wound in Savage's chest.

It felt like forever before the paramedics arrived, but I knew realistically it had only been a few minutes. We moved to the side so they could get to Savage, and then

Nick scooped me up in his arms and held me while we watched them work.

"I'm glad you came when you did," I said. "I was starting to get worried."

"You took ten years off my life when I saw you slide into that hallway. Please don't do that again."

I wasn't sure how long we sat there and watched the paramedics work. Someone came up and put a blanket around me. I guess I was shivering—the blood soaking my dress had turned cold..

"We've got him," one of the paramedics called out. "Pulse and blood pressure are steady. Let's move him."

They put him on a stretcher and a cry hitched in my throat as he held up a hand. He was awake. I scrambled out of Nick's arms and moved over to him. Nick was right beside me.

I grabbed his hand after they got him on the gurney and he opened his eyes to look at me.

"You're a mess," he said, and I burst into tears.

"Did I ruin the wedding?" he asked.

"You tried," I said.

He almost smiled.

"We've got to move him," the EMT said.

I nodded and tried to let go of his hand, but he held on tight. And then he looked right at Nick. "You're a lucky man," he said. "She's a good partner."

Nick nodded and tears streamed down my face. "It's been a pleasure, Addison Holmes. If you're ever in South Dakota, come by for a visit."

"South Dakota?" Nick asked as they wheeled him away.

"Boy, have I got a lot to tell you." I threw my arms around him and hugged him tight.

Chapter Twenty-One

I'M NOT sure how much time passed before we were moved to a different location. The party was still going strong outside. I could hear the crowd and wondered if they'd even been aware of what had happened.

I must have been in a state of shock, because Nick leaned down and said, "Do you still want to get married tonight?"

I did. I really did.

I nodded and he said, "Wait here."

Before too long had passed Rosemarie came bustling in. I'd forgotten she was dressed like Kim Jong Un, so it was a little startling to see. Several agents gave her a wide berth as she steam-rolled toward them. She was carrying something in her hands.

"Yikes," she said, looking me over. "It's like a stage production of Sweeney Todd in here. It's just terrible what happened to Savage. I heard he saved that agent's life. Jumped right in front of him and shoved him to the ground."

News traveled fast. I'd just been told that from the agent whose life he saved.

"Nick said the wedding was still on," she continued. "Come on. We've got to make you presentable."

She pushed me toward the back of the church, behind the sanctuary where there was a small changing area behind the baptismal. Kate and my mother came right in behind us, carrying a trash bag full of something.

"What's all that?" I asked.

"I'm a wedding planner," Rosemarie said. "I always have a backup plan. Or at least I will once I start my own business. I'm learning from experience right now, so I'm making things up as I go along. The good news is I figure if I can make this wedding come off without a hitch then there's nothing I can't tackle. This wedding is a doozy."

My mother pulled out a pair of her sewing sheers and came toward me. If I hadn't just been through a traumatic experience I probably could've dodged out of her way faster.

"Hold still," she said. And then she cut my dress from the bosom all the way to the hem. The blood had started to dry in places, so the dress was stuck to me, and she and Kate tugged from each side until I was standing naked.

"I'd like to reach a point in my life where I stop being naked in front of people. When does that happen?"

"My mom snorted out a laugh. You're a woman. That never happens. Wait until you have children. You're all sprawled out on the delivery table, and complete strangers are walking in looking at your bits. When Phoebe was born there was an observation class of twenty men watching me. I swear half of them had never seen a naked woman before and the other half couldn't grow facial hair."

"That's nothing," Rosemarie said. "I had hemorrhoid surgery a few years back. Most painful thing I've ever done. By the time I went back for my post-op I was stripping out of my clothes walking through the waiting room of doctor's office. He didn't even have to ask me to crawl up on the table of all fours. I would've done it in the checkout line at Walmart if it meant getting some of that numbing cream."

Kate had stayed silent and she had a thoughtful look on her face.

"What?" I asked.

"That's a lot of blood," she said, looking me up and down. "You're covered in it."

"It's not like I've got a shower on hand."

"Weeellll," Kate said, looking slightly apologetic.

"Oh," Rosemarie said. "Oh, my." And then she crossed herself.

I didn't know what was happening, but I didn't like the looks I was getting. The three women came at me all at once, and they pushed me toward the narrow stairs that led up to the baptistery.

And then I stepped off into empty space and plunged into cold water. I came up sputtering. "Are you kidding me? I can't bathe in the baptismal? I'm covered in blood."

"Now that you mention it," Rosemarie said, crossing herself again. "It seems kind of fitting. But just in case, why don't you hurry and get out."

"It's freezing," I said, teeth chattering as I made my way over to the ladder.

"Here," my mother said. She'd managed to find the stash of choir robes somewhere and draped it over my shoulders.

"Wow," Rosemarie said, looking into the baptismal. "That's a lot of blood."

"Yeah," Kate said. "I didn't think the water would turn red like that."

"Maybe they'll think it's wine," my mother said. "Come on. We don't have all night. Those people out there are getting antsy. They won't serve from the cake and ice cream truck until y'all get married. There will be riots soon."

They ushered me back into the changing area. My skin was pebbled and I couldn't stop shaking.

"Damn," Kate said. "That airbrush stuff really works. It still looks like it was just applied. That can't be healthy for you."

"Did everyone bring the backup clothes?" Rosemarie asked. "This is desperate times and desperate measures."

My mom and Kate dumped out the trash bag they'd brought in, and out fell a pile of clothes.

"We had to scrounge what we could get in the clothes department," my mom said. She held up a square of denim and a plaid shirt. "Nina Dempsey said you could wear her overalls. She brought them just in case."

"That woman is all heart," Rosemarie said. "What else is there? Did you look in my trunk?"

"Yes," Kate said. "And we'll talk about that later. We found your emergency overnight bag of clothes. Nothing in there will fit Addison."

"What about my Snuggie?" she asked. "That's one-size-fits all."

"It's also open in the back like a hospital gown," my mother said. "There's already one full moon out tonight. We don't need to see another."

"But it's white," Rosemarie said. "And it's got pockets."

I wasn't sure what pockets had to do with anything, but the one things I did know was Snuggies were warm. And I wasn't.

"Let's do it," I said.

"I've got an idea," Rosemarie said, and she ran over to the closet where my mom had gotten the choir and baptismal robes. In another cabinet were the stoles Pastor Charles would wear when he was baptizing someone.

"It's black," she said. "But I hear people wear black to weddings now days."

They wrapped me in the white Snuggie and wrapped the

stole around my waist several times before tucking the stray ends underneath.

"What do you think?" I asked.

"I think you're going to get frostbite on your lady bits," Kate said. "You've still got a lot of real estate showing back there."

"I've got safety pins," my mother said, rummaging through her bag. "I've always told you girls to carry an emergency sewing kit with you. This just proves my point."

It proved the point that in more than thirty years of life, I'd needed an emergency sewing kit once. The odds were in my favor. But I was glad she had it.

She finished sewing me up, and I was pleasantly surprised with the final outcome. It wasn't great, but it could've been a lot worse.

Kate was looking back and forth between me and Rose-marie. "I feel like we're about to go to a meeting of fascist dictators."

Nick knocked on the door and said, "How'd it go? Are you ready?" And then he caught sight of me. "Interesting choice."

"It was this or your mother's overalls."

"She's always thinking of others," he said, and then he held out his hand.

He led me out of the church and we made our way toward the distillery. The sea of people parted for us this time and there were cheers as they realized the wedding was about to take place.

"They're excited about the cake and ice cream truck. We had to put an extra security detail around it because people were starting to get violent. The booze truck has already run out. My grandfather sent for two more."

"He's a smart man," I said.

"Yes, he was smart enough to bring his own bottle and avoid the lines."

Rosemarie was already waiting at the top of the steps for us, her bible in hand.

"She reminds me of someone," Nick said, and then he snapped his fingers. "I've got it. She looks like Dr. Evil."

"Come on, you two," Rosemarie called out. "I can smell the Italian buffet inside the distillery, and I need some lasagna in the worst way. You have no idea how hard it is to trick all these people into believing they didn't hear gunshots."

"How'd you accomplish that?" I asked.

"Because I'm a wedding planner. We plan for *everything*. When the agents and cops started running, no one paid much attention. But I knew some heavy stuff was about to go down when they moved Nick's grandfather inside. As soon as the gunfire started I had the foresight to start the fireworks. It was really spectacular. It's a shame you had to miss the show. And no one knew what was really going on."

"Fireworks?" I asked. "Why did you plan for fireworks?"

"I figured it would be nicer to leave to fireworks exploding in the sky than being pelted with rice and birdseed. That shit hurts."

Rosemarie held up her hands to silence the crowd. I was surprised it worked, but I figured everyone was probably confused why she was starting our wedding ceremony like it was the beginning of the Hunger Games.

Kate was to my left and Mike, Kate's husband, was standing next to Nick as his best man. Despite the contentiousness of our two families, everyone was there, standing on each side of us as we were about to make a lifelong commitment—everyone but Scarlet—but I knew she was there in spirit. In the end, we might disagree, or get fed up with each other, or even hate each other at times. But we were family.

"Dearly, beloved—" Rosemarie began, her voice loud and strong.

"Hold on a sec," I told her, and then I turned to look at Nick. I was going to tell him about the baby. I swear I was. But at the last second I chickened out. "I just wanted to say I love you," I told him.

He looked at me kind of strange and then gave me a half-smile. "I love you, too."

"Dearly, beloved—" Rosemarie said again.

"Sorry," I said. "I just need another minute." I turned back to Nick. "We've never really talked about having children.

Do you like them? Are you opposed to them? What if we get some and we end up not liking them?"

The people around us were leaning in so they could hear what I was saying, and then I heard the whispers run through the crowd as the news traveled from person to person like a game of telephone.

Nick's brows raised. "You want to talk about this now?" he asked.

"It seems like an important topic to discuss before marriage," I said. "And we're right here before marriage, so…" I swallowed hard. "So I thought we should talk about it."

"Okay," Nick said, patiently. "I think I'd like to have children someday. And I'd especially like making them with you."

I felt the heat rise to my cheeks. "What about if we don't like them or we're not good at being parents."

"Addison," he said. "Relax. Think how many times our parents screwed us up, and we turned out okay. We'll be great. And if one of them turns out to be like Aunt Scarlet we can always ship her off to France."

I nodded and tried to smile. I was nervous. I just needed to tell him. Instead, I turned back to Rosemarie and said, "We're ready."

"Nothing like waiting until the last minute to discuss big ticket items," she said. And then she looked at me pointedly, knowing I was a big chicken. But I didn't stop her again.

"Dearly, beloved—" she said for the third time.

The ceremony was a blur. I knew she was speaking, and I knew I must have said all the right things in the right places, but I couldn't have told you what was being said. Before I knew it, Nick was leaning down to kiss me and a roar of applause and cheers sounded behind us.

When he finally let me go, I was out of breath, and I was pretty sure my Snuggie had come undone in a couple of places. Nick was a very powerful kisser.

He was smiling, and I said, "I'm pregnant."

I didn't say it loud, but it was certainly loud enough for him to hear.

"Did you seriously wait until we were married before you told me that?" he asked.

"Scarlet said men get skittish about pregnancy. I wanted to make sure you were locked in. Or as least where I could legally take half your fortune if you decided to bail."

His lips twitched and he pulled me into him again. "You're serious?" he asked. "About the baby, I mean."

"Yes, little Scarlet could be in there cooking as we speak."

"Why are you trying to scare me off?" he asked. "I already married you. I'm stuck with you for the long haul. And you're stuck with me."

He had a funny look on his face, and I wondered what was going on. I had too many emotions running through me to be able to think straight. "There's no one I'd rather be stuck with."

"Good," he said. "Because I think that having kids and working cop hours aren't the best thing for a family."

"What?" I asked. "I thought you loved being a cop."

"I do. But I love other things more. Like you. And little Scarlet."

"You've got to stop calling her that. You're going to jinx us." I was in a complete state of shock. I'd never thought of Nick doing anything else. "What would you do instead?"

"There's been a Dempsey in the senate for a lot of years, and my grandfather is about to retire. I was thinking it might be good to stick with tradition."

I arched a brow and said, "Did you seriously wait until we were married before you told me that?"

He shrugged. "Too late. You're not going anywhere now."

"As long as I'm with you I'm happy," I said. "I don't care if you're a cop or a senator. Or if we have twenty little Scarlets."

"Tap the brakes there," he said, wincing.

"This is the start of a new chapter in our lives. And hopefully it's going to start with cake because I haven't been able to think of anything else since I last ate it." And then I remembered what Nick's cake looked like. "We'll start with the bride's cake. You haven't had enough to drink to hack off a piece of yours yet."

He looked confused. He was probably going to get that look several times throughout the reception. I hadn't told him about the band from the strip club.

"After you, Mrs. Dempsey," he said, holding the door of the distillery open for me. "All new chapters, at least the good ones, should start with cake."

Yep. He was definitely the right one."

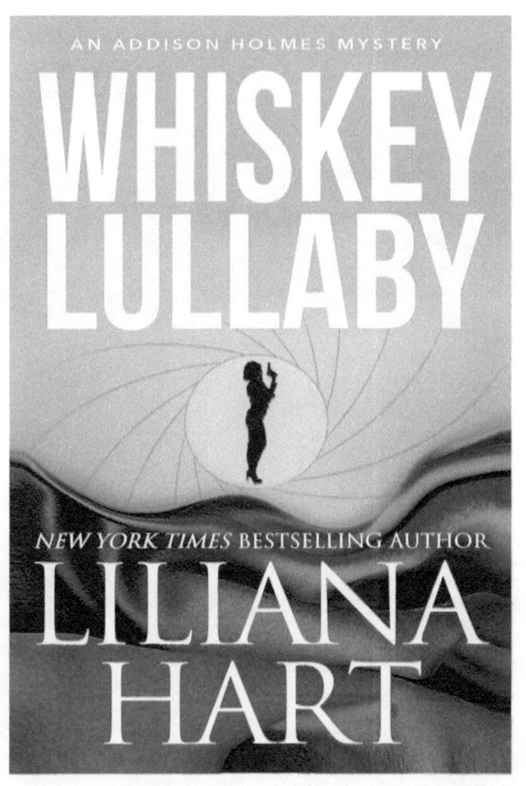

The Adventure Continues for Addison Holmes.

Excerpt - JJ Graves Mystery Series

Discover Liliana Hart's bestselling J.J. Graves mystery series. *DIRTY LITTLE SECRETS* is available at all retailers!

Fourth generation mortician. That's a lot of dead bodies.

I thought I'd be proud to carry on the family legacy, but that was before I knew the job would be hell on my social life. I mean, who wanted to date a woman who drained blood on a regular basis and whose scent of choice was embalming fluid?

Sure, I got a little lonely sometimes. It mostly happened when I was preparing a body in the middle of the night instead of snuggled up next to someone warm with a pulse. But dead bodies were my business. And I hated every fucking minute of it. I never wanted to take over the family funeral parlor. I wanted to be a doctor. Well, technically, I *was* a doctor, but I preferred to be one for the living.

My parents died early last year, and the gossip and scandal involved would have broken someone with a lesser constitution, but I'd managed to hold my head up. Mostly. It was because of my parents that I'd had an impromptu career change. The only thing I had left of them was the crumbling old Victorian I grew up in and Graves Funeral Home —believe me, it was a hell of a legacy.

I had little choice but to resign my job at the hospital, pack my bags and move back to Bloody Mary, Virginia—population 2,902. The good thing about owning a funeral home in Bloody Mary was that hardly anyone ever died, despite the rather macabre name. The bad thing about it was I had a shitload of student loans to pay back and not a lot of income.

Did I mention the budget cuts?

Ahh, my life was simple before the budget cuts. The mayor's decision to be more fiscally conservative left King George County without a coroner. So, I, J.J. Graves, in a moment of temporary insanity, volunteered for the job. In all actuality, I was strong-armed into taking the position out of a sense of duty to the community and the guilt of tarnishing my family's good name. Well, tarnishing it any more than it already was.

Which brought me here. Alone in my bed in the middle of the night. My bedroom so cold white puffs of breath clouded above my face every time I exhaled because I couldn't afford to crank the heater above 65 degrees. My toes wiggled and fought for release beneath the nubby covers I'd tucked under the mattress too snugly, and goose bumps spread across the top of my skull and tightened the skin so much that it felt as if the follicles might snap off.

I'd been wide-awake for more than an hour, thinking of my family, what was left of my legacy, and how much my life in general sucked. Not for the first time, the thought entered my mind that it wouldn't be so terrible if I just packed a bag and left everything behind me without a word to anyone. I didn't have any family to worry over my disappearance. No children to leave belongings to. Sure, my friends would miss me for a while. But eventually the people who'd watched me grow up would only have passing thoughts about that Graves' girl whose parents killed themselves. All the while I would be starting a new life. Hopefully someplace warm.

But like I always did, I immediately dismissed the thought. It took more courage than I had to start over and leave everything familiar behind. I needed something in my life besides a half-assed career and a mountain of debt. A man would be nice. A man who'd be willing to have sex would be even better. But chances of that happening were somewhere between negative four and zero. Not because Bloody Mary didn't have its fair share of men, but because I was just picky. Bloody Mary wasn't exactly teeming with single males under the age of forty who had health insurance and all their own teeth.

I huffed out another white puff of breath and rolled over, punching my pillow and clearing my mind of all thoughts that didn't involve counting sheep. I'd had trouble sleeping since I'd moved home. Maybe it was because the house was empty and made weird noises and my imagination assumed the cold blasts of air and the rattling pipes were the haunts of all my ancestors shaking their heads in pity. Or maybe it was because the mattress was old and lumpy. Who the hell knew? But I'd learned to function on just a few hours of sleep when I was in medical school, so I was used to having bags under my eyes and skin that looked like it never saw the light of day.

The silence of the house smothered me—a heap of decaying wood and rotting shingles that crushed me with the weight of neglect and responsibility—so I burrowed under the covers, searching for peace of mind and the comfortable spot on the mattress that always seemed to elude me. I'd almost talked myself into getting up and starting a pot of coffee when the phone warbled on the bedside table.

I cursed out a mumbled, "Shit" in surprise and flailed under the covers so my sheets resembled something along the lines of a straitjacket. My pulse jumped and throbbed in the side of my neck, and each pounding beat marched through the synapses of my brain until I became lightheaded with something I recognized as fear. I closed my eyes and let out a slow breath.

The only time I got calls in the middle of the night was when someone died. I hated death. I hated that my parents had left such a massive responsibility on my shoulders. And most of all I hated that I was the only one the dead could turn to. I missed the living. The dead made me think of too many things I wasn't quite ready to face.

Against my better judgment, I answered the phone.

"Who died?"

"Very professional, Doctor Graves," said Sheriff Jack Lawson. "You always assume the worst. What if I was calling to invite you to poker tonight at my place?"

"At five o'clock in the morning? Who died?" I asked again. Jack had been my best friend since we'd been in diapers, and I knew without a doubt he'd be the one person who'd search for me if I just disappeared one day. I squeezed the phone in a white knuckled grasp as silence reigned on the other end of the line. I prepared myself for the worst.

"It's Fiona Murphy," he finally said.

"Oh, damn," I whispered, untangling the covers and sitting up on the side of the bed. The wood floor felt like a sheet of ice under my feet, and I drew them up quickly so they were back under the covers.

"To say the least." Sirens and muted voices came across the line, and I knew Jack must be at the crime scene.

My teeth chattered—I couldn't tell if it was from the news or the cold—and I gritted them in determination so my words came out clearly. "Where's George?"

George was Fiona's husband. He was the meanest son of a bitch I'd ever met, and Fiona had a new bruise every time I saw her. George was a gifted mechanic and owned the only garage in town, so despite people disapproving of the way he treated his wife, he had a hell of a customer base and enough money to build a house that was one of the nicest in the county. He also had big hands and a wicked temper, and there wasn't a doubt in my mind he was the reason Fiona was dead at age thirty.

"George has already been picked up and booked on a first degree murder charge. We need you down at the site. The crime scene guys are almost finished. I'm warning you, Jaye, she doesn't look good. Johnny Duggan found her in the ditch just off Canterbury Street on his way to work."

I swallowed the lump in my throat and prayed to a God I'd stopped believing in for strength. "I can handle it, Jack. I'm all she's got." It was the least I could do for a dead friend.

Bloody Mary—Population 2,901.

About the Author

Liliana Hart is a New York Times, USAToday, and Publisher's Weekly bestselling author of more than sixty titles. After starting her first novel her freshman year of college, she immediately became addicted to writing and knew she'd found what she was meant to do with her life. She has no idea why she majored in music.

Since publishing in June 2011, Liliana has sold more than six-million books. All three of her series have made multiple appearances on the New York Times list.

Liliana can almost always be found at her computer writing, hauling five kids to various activities, or spending time with her husband. She calls Texas home.

If you enjoyed reading *this*, I would appreciate it if you would help others enjoy this book, too.

 Lend it. This e-book is lending-enabled, so please, share it with a friend.

Recommend it. Please help other readers find this book by recommending it to friends, readers' groups and discussion boards.

Review it. Please tell other readers why you liked this book by reviewing. If you do write a review, please send me an email at lilianahartauthor@gmail.com, or visit me at http://www.lilianahart.com.

Connect with me online:
www.lilianahart.com
lilianahartauthor@gmail.com

facebook.com/LilianaHart
x.com/Liliana_Hart
instagram.com/LilianaHart
bookbub.com/authors/liliana-hart

JJ Graves Mystery Series

Dirty Little Secrets

A Dirty Shame

Dirty Rotten Scoundrel

Down and Dirty

Dirty Deeds

Dirty Laundry

Dirty Money

A Dirty Job

Dirty Devil

Playing Dirty

Dirty Martini

Dirty Dozen

Dirty Minds

Dirty Weekend

Dirty Looks

Dirty Liars

Dirty Valentine

Addison Holmes Mystery Series

Whiskey Rebellion

Whiskey Sour

Whiskey For Breakfast

Whiskey, You're The Devil

Whiskey on the Rocks

Whiskey Tango Foxtrot

Whiskey and Gunpowder

Whiskey Lullaby

The Scarlet Chronicles

Bouncing Betty

Hand Grenade Helen

Front Line Francis

The Harley and Davidson Mystery Series

The Farmer's Slaughter

A Tisket a Casket

I Saw Mommy Killing Santa Claus

Get Your Murder Running

Deceased and Desist

Malice in Wonderland

Tequila Mockingbird

Gone With the Sin

Grime and Punishment

Blazing Rattles

A Salt and Battery

Curl Up and Dye

First Comes Death Then Comes Marriage

Box Set 1

Box Set 2

Box Set 3

The Gravediggers

The Darkest Corner

Gone to Dust

Say No More

Laurel Valley

Tribulation Pass

Redemption Road

Midnight Clear

Forgiveness River

Atonement Trail